COLD AS STONE

STONEHEART MOTORCYCLE CLUB
BOOK 3

EVIE MITCHELL

THUNDER THIGHS PUBLISHING

Editor: Nicole McCurdy, Emerald Edits
https://www.emeraldedits.com/

Editor: Aquila Editing
http://www.aquilaediting.com/

Cover design: Megan Wade
Map design: Evie Mitchell
Images: Deposit Photo

To all those starting over.

May you find your home and happiness.

And to Rooks.

Always.

ACKNOWLEDGEMENT OF COUNTRY

I acknowledge the Traditional Custodians of the lands on which I write, the Ngunnawal people, and pay my respect to elders both past and present.

I acknowledge the continued and deep spiritual relationship of the Australian Aboriginal and Torres Strait Islander peoples' to this land, and their unique cultural and spiritual relationships to the land, waters and seas, and their rich contribution to society.

Always was, always will be.

CONTENT INFORMATION

Please note the following content information include
SPOILERS for this book.

SPOILERS BELOW

Themes

This story contains references to loss of a parent, grief, car
accident/incident, drunk driving references, abandonment,
poverty, loneliness, alcohol abuse, threats, violence.

Includes swearing, and consensual but explicit sexual
scenes.

More information

If you have any concerns with the depictions in this story or
would like further information before reading, please email
Evie@EvieMitchell.com

END SPOILERS

COLD AS STONE

She came back to bury her past. He's been waiting to claim his future.

KYA

I swore I'd never set foot in Stoneheart again. But here I am, sorting through the wreckage of my mother's life—and the lottery ticket worth a million dollars she left behind.

I was ready to leave as quickly as I arrived… until I saw *him.*

Lee Armstrong. My best friend's brother. The boy I've loved since I was twelve.

I came back to settle an estate. I didn't expect to buy the local dive bar. And I certainly didn't expect to start falling for the man who looks at me like I'm both temptation and trouble.

LEE

Kya walking back into my life was the last thing I saw coming. One look and I'm ruined. She was my little sister's best friend, but now I want her in every way.

But her decision to buy the local dive bar has painted a target on her back. Summit Development doesn't mess about — they use bruisers and intimidation. As the Stoneheart Motorcycle Club's enforcer I'm used to dealing with threats. I can stop bullets and bulldozers, but I can't force her to stay. Getting Kya to believe she's safe , and that she's the only woman I want, is a fight I never expected.

Cold as Stone *is a steamy, emotional motorcycle club romance featuring a heroine learning to accept love from her best friend's brother, a possessive hero who's been waiting for his chance, and a small town fighting for its soul. With themes of homecoming, healing from trauma, and finding family in unexpected places, this story delivers passion, protection, and second chances.*

If you love heroines who don't know their own worth, patient heroes who excel at both dirty talk and emotional support, and a found family of bikers who take bets on everything, this book is for you!

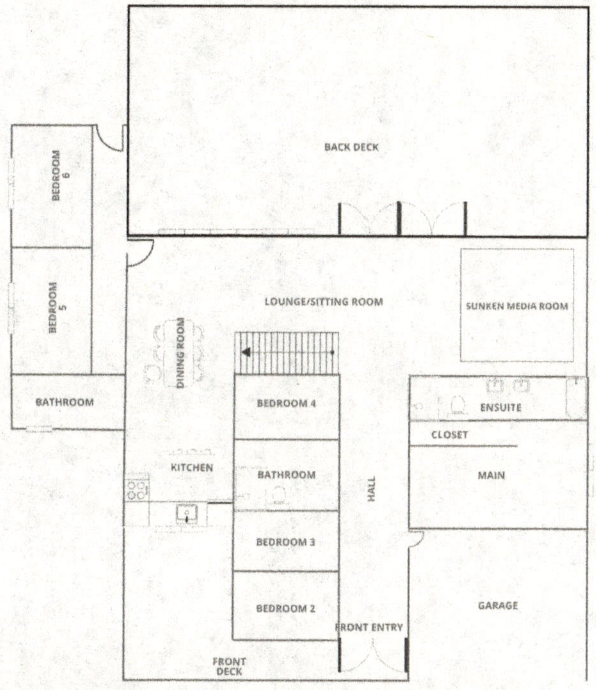

THE CLUB HOUSE
GROUND LEVEL

4 Acres
Land

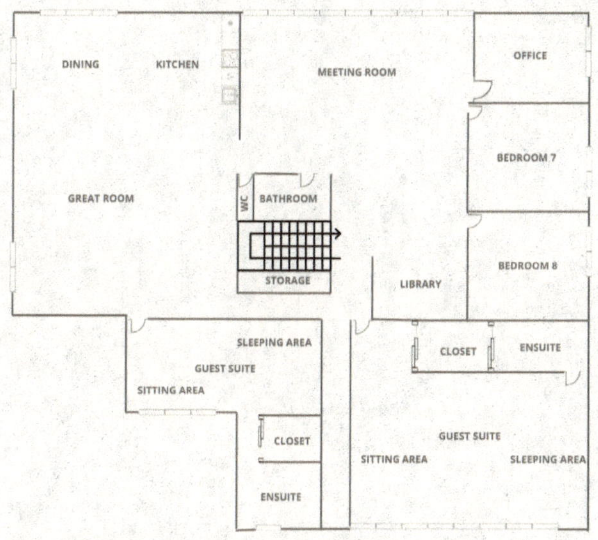

THE CLUB HOUSE

UPPER LEVEL

4 Acres
Land

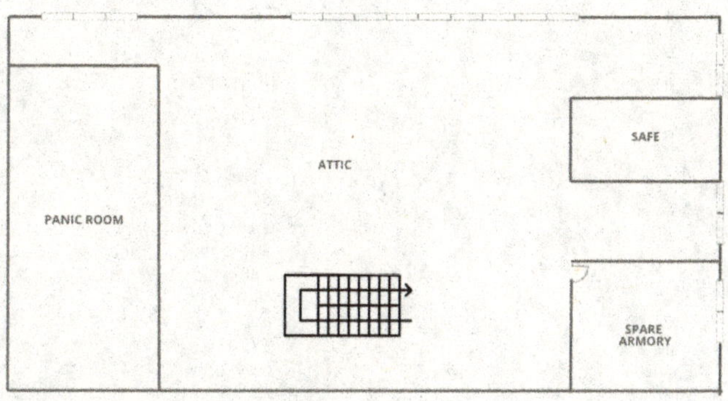

THE CLUB HOUSE
ATTIC

4 Acres
Land

THE CHAPEL

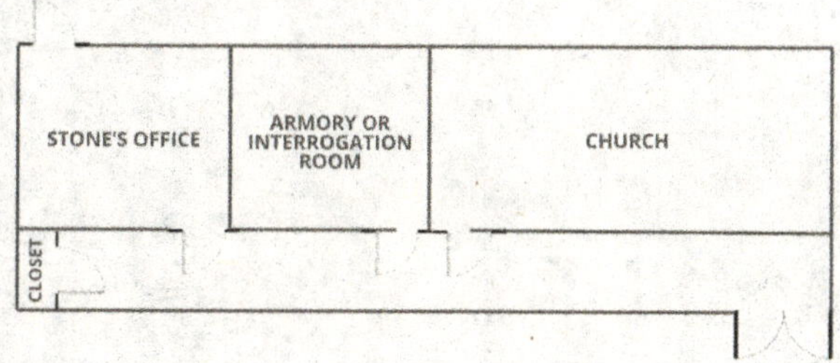

THE BARRACKS
GROUND FLOOR

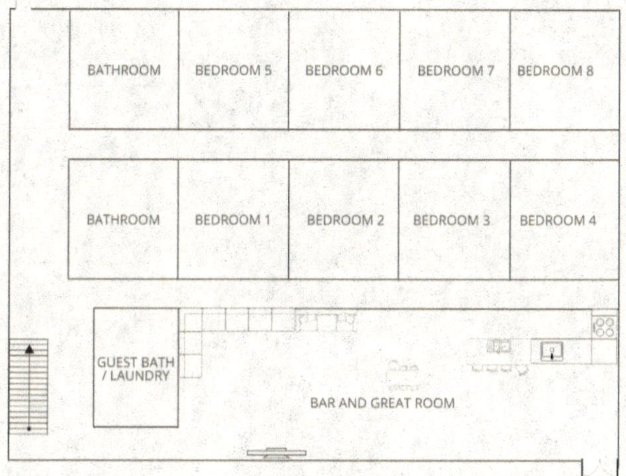

THE BARRACKS
LEVEL 1

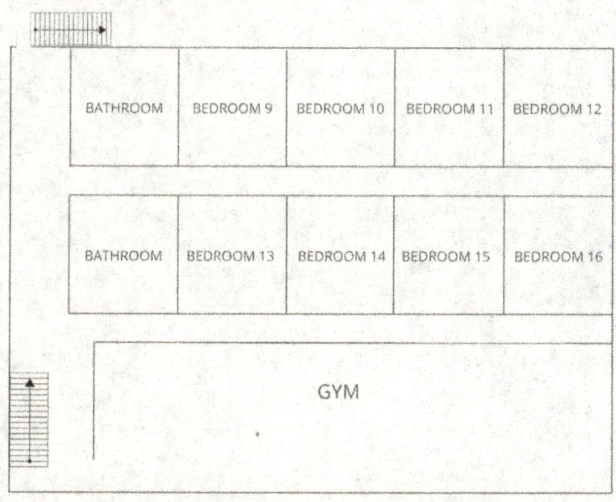

THE BARRACKS
LEVEL 2

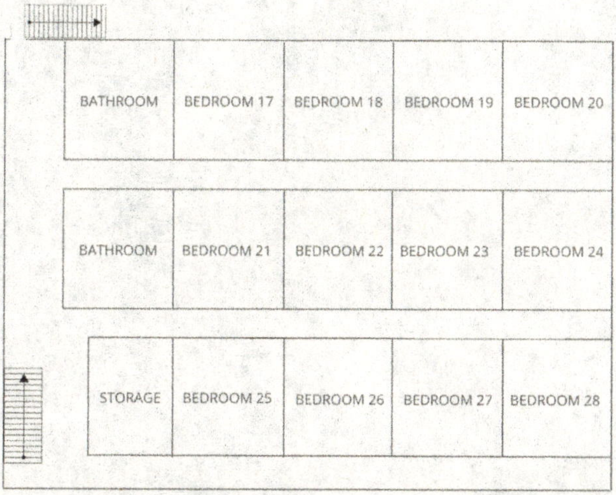

PROLOGUE
KYA

Faster! Keep running!

The unexpected sleet cuts through the October air like tiny glass shards, each drop a frozen needle against my skin. My pajamas—a faded pink shirt a size too small, and long leggings with a raggedy hole in one knee—cling to my body like wet tissue paper. The thin cotton does nothing against the cold that seeps into my bones, but I don't stop.

Can't stop.

My lungs burn with each ragged breath, the frigid air slicing through my throat like broken glass. Every inhale is a struggle, choppy and painful, but I force myself to keep going. My stomach churns with terror, twisted into knots so tight I taste bile. The panic claws at my insides, making my hands shake and my vision blur at the edges, but the fear of what's behind me is stronger than the fear of what's ahead.

The cracked sidewalk bites at my bare feet with each slapping step, and I taste copper in my mouth where I've bitten my tongue. The street lights blur past in streaks of yellow, like fallen stars smeared across my vision. Houses huddle behind their neat little fences, windows glowing amber and gold. Here, on the richer side of town, families rest safely inside their perfect little homes.

It's only a few miles from my own run-down trailer, and yet it's a world away from the dank, dirty, and dangerous place I just fled.

The image of him—reeking breath, hand tightening around my wrist—flares in my mind like a flashbang. I shove it down, deeper.

Keep moving.

My pulse stutters wildly, hammering against my ribs like a trapped bird. Nausea churns in my gut, bile rising to coat my mouth with a bitter burn. The memory sends ice through my veins even as my skin burns with shame and terror. I shove it down, deeper.

Don't think. Hurry!

I take a sharp left, nearly slipping as my foot hits a slick patch of leaves. The sleet's coming harder now, icy needles lashing my face. But I see it. Emma's house.

My feet carry me down the frozen sidewalk, past the park where we'd swing until our legs ached and talk about all the places we'd go together when we grew up.

That was before she left and everything changed.

Tears streak down my cheeks, blending with the sleet.

Fuck. I'm still here, trapped, counting down the days until

my eighteenth birthday when I can finally escape this hell. Nine months, two weeks and three days.

The porch light's on, music thumping inside, laughter spilling out into the storm like it's just another Friday night. Motorcycles line the driveway—big, chrome beasts that gleam even in the dim streetlight. Harley-Davidsons mostly, with a few others I don't recognize.

This isn't the house I remember. Emma's house was quiet, filled with the smell of her mom's lavender candles and the sound of classical music drifting from the piano in the front room. This house thrums with masculine energy, all leather and motor oil and something darker that makes my pulse skip.

But I don't have anywhere else to go.

The ancient oak that Emma and I climbed a thousand times is gone. Just a stump now, surrounded by sawdust that's turned to mud in the rain. We used to shimmy up its thick trunk to Emma's second-story window, spending countless nights whispering secrets and planning our futures. She was going to be a prima ballerina. I was going to do anything that made me enough money to get out of this hick town. We were going to be best friends forever.

I was so stupid.

Now I stand at the front door like a stranger, my hand shaking as I touch the knob. The porch light flickers, casting dancing shadows across the worn wooden planks.

It's a party. I'll just slip in and hide in the crush. If I can get to Emma's room, I'll be safe. It's just for the night. One night. No one will even know I've been here.

The music pounds through the door, and I can hear voices —deep, rough laughter that makes something in my stomach flutter with nerves. These aren't the high school or college boys who hang around the diner where I work. These are men. Real men, with callused hands and scars and stories I probably don't want to know.

But it's too late to run now. I'm soaked through and shivering so hard my teeth sound like castanets. If I don't get warm soon, I'll collapse right here on the porch.

I go to turn the knob, but the door is already opening. Warm air rushes out to greet me, carrying the scents of beer and cigarettes and something else—leather and motor oil and soap.

I stumble, nearly face-planting into a wall of muscle.

A wall of Harley "Lee" Armstrong. Emma's older brother.

The original bad boy blueprint.

I nursed the biggest crush on him. The can't-breathe, can't-speak, write-his-name-in-the-margins-of-your-math-book kind.

But I never told anyone.

Not even Emma. *Especially* not Emma.

Lee had that lazy, untouchable energy that made you wonder if he even *knew* how attractive he was—or if he just didn't care. He'd always been tall, lean, and ridiculously good-looking. Half the girls in our grade had dated him, and the other half had wished we were able to.

He had this way of looking *through* people, not cruel, just... unreachable. But every now and then, you'd catch his attention and it would be on you—completely. I lived for those moments, when he'd flash his sideways smirk, lazy and amused, seemingly impressed that you could engage his attention.

He could have easily been an ass, but for some reason that wasn't who Lee was. He was the kind of guy who always slid me the last piece of pizza, seemingly knowing I was starving but too polite to take it. He'd been Emma's champion, carrying her backpack when it was too heavy, and warning her about guys who weren't good enough for his little sis.

He had this way of being quietly protective without making a big deal about it. Like the time Danny Morrison was giving me grief about being trailer trash. Lee just... appeared. He hadn't said a word. Just stood there, all six-foot-two of controlled danger. Danny hadn't bothered me again.

But when he got mad—really mad—it was like watching a summer storm. Not wild or explosive. Just focused. Controlled. Terrifying in the way distant thunder is, because you *know* the storm is coming, and you know it's going to be biblical.

But that boy? He's long gone.

My gaze drifts up, noting that he's filled out, his shoulders now broad enough to block the porch light. His dark hair is shorter, military-neat but long enough on top that it falls across his forehead. A few days' worth of stubble shadows his jaw, and there's a hardness in his eyes that was never there before.

But it's the leather cut stretched across his chest that stops me cold. *Stoneheart MC* arcs across his shoulders in bold white letters. *Prospect* is patched beneath it, marking him as someone working to earn membership in the club.

Damn and double damn.

Lee's eyes go wide as they take me in. My soaked clothes cling to every curve of my too-abundant body. My bare feet burn with cold, and I'm painfully aware that I'm shaking so hard I can barely stand.

"Shit." His voice is deeper than I remember, rougher around the edges. "Kya?"

The sound of my name on his lips hits me like a physical blow. I haven't heard it said with anything approaching tenderness in so long that I almost start crying right there on his doorstep.

Instead, I turn away. "Sorry. I shouldn't have—this was stupid. I'll just—"

His hand closes around my arm before I can take a step, firm but gentle. His skin is warm against mine, and I can feel the calluses on his palm, the strength in his fingers.

"Whoa. Stop." He tugs me back around to face him, his brow furrowed with concern. "What the hell happened to you?"

I open my mouth to answer, but nothing comes out. My jaw won't work right, my teeth chattering too hard to form words. All I can do is stand there and shake like a leaf in a hurricane while he studies my face with those penetrating green eyes.

"Christ," he mutters, and then his hand is on my back, guiding me through the door. "You're frozen solid. Come on."

The warmth inside hits me like a wall, and I gasp at the sudden change in temperature. The house is full of noise and bodies—men in leather cuts clustered around the kitchen island, a few women in tight jeans and barely-there tops draped over various pieces of furniture. Someone's playing pool, the crack of balls echoing over the music.

They all turn to look when Lee guides me inside, and I want to disappear. I'm acutely aware of how I must look like a drowned racoon. Next to these put-together women with their perfect hair and confident smiles, I feel like exactly what I am, a scared little girl.

But Lee doesn't seem to notice their stares. He keeps his hand on my back, steering me toward the stairs.

"Lee?" one of the men calls out—a guy with graying temples and a patch I can't quite make out on his cut. He's older than most of the men in the room, more weathered, but his eyes are kind when they land on me. "Everything alright?"

"Yeah, Duck. Just taking care of something." Lee's voice is carefully neutral, but there's an edge to it that makes the other man nod and turn back to his conversation.

The stairs creak under our combined weight as Lee guides me up, his hand never leaving my back. The hallway at the top is dimmer, lit only by a small lamp on a side table. Family photos line the walls showing Emma at various dance recitals, Lee in his military dress uniform, the whole family at some long-ago Christmas.

He pushes open the bathroom door and flips on the heat lights.

"Shower. Now." His tone brooks no argument. "Hot as you can stand it. I'll grab you some clothes."

I nod mutely, still too cold and shocked to protest. He starts to leave, then pauses in the doorway.

"Kya." His voice is softer now, almost gentle. "You're safe here. Okay?"

I nod again, not trusting my voice.

The door clicks shut behind him, and I'm alone with the sound of my own chattering teeth and the hum of the lights. I catch sight of myself in the mirror above the sink and wince. I look exactly as bad as I thought—pale and pinched, my lips nearly blue, with dark circles under my eyes.

The shower is a godsend. I step under the spray fully clothed, letting the hot water pound against my skin until feeling starts to return to my extremities. It hurts at first, pins and needles shooting through my hands and feet, but gradually the warmth seeps deeper, loosening the knots in my muscles.

I peel off the sodden clothes and let them fall to the shower floor with a wet slap. The water runs pink for a moment where my feet were bleeding. I must have cut them on the rough pavement.

Damn. That's gonna hurt tomorrow.

I let myself sink down onto the shower floor, arms wrapped around my knees. The hot water streams over my head, washing away the last of the panic and leaving behind something else, a hollow ache in my chest that I'm afraid to examine too closely.

I can't go home. I don't have money. I don't have a plan. I don't even have shoes. God. What am I doing?

I'm seventeen, half naked in my former best friend's brother's bathroom.

This is insane.

And yet... I don't regret coming here. Not for a second, because for the first time all night, I feel safe.

I step out of the shower as there's a soft knock on the door.

"I'm leaving some stuff by the door," Lee calls through the wood. "Hoodie, sweats. They'll drown you, but they're dry."

"Thank you," I manage to croak out.

"Take your time."

I wrap myself in a towel as I hear his footsteps retreat down the hall. When I open the door, I find the promised clothes folded neatly outside the door. The hoodie is massive, navy blue with *Stoneheart MC* embroidered on the front in silver thread. It hangs to mid-thigh, the sleeves covering my hands completely. The sweatpants are equally oversized, soft gray cotton that I have to roll up three times at the ankles.

They smell like him—soap and smoke and something indefinably masculine. I bury my face in the fabric and breathe deeply.

You're pathetic. You know that, right?

Shaking off my momentary insanity, I pad down the hallway, wincing as my feet protest.

The party has clearly wound down. The music is off, and most of the people I saw earlier are gone. Only a few remain, clustered around the kitchen island with bottles of beer and serious expressions. They look up when I appear in the doorway, and I freeze under their collective gaze.

Heat floods my cheeks at how I must look drowning in Lee's oversized clothes. It's embarrassing that they see me for who I am, a desperate girl with nowhere else to go.

I force myself to lift my chin, meeting each stare head-on. Whatever judgment they're passing, whatever assumptions they're making—I won't give them the satisfaction of seeing me cower. This shame isn't mine to carry.

Or so I tell myself.

Lee sits on the edge of the couch, elbows on his knees, hands clasped in front of him. When he sees me, he straightens, and something in his expression shifts.

"Come here," he says, his voice low and steady.

I do, my bare feet silent on the hardwood floor. The other men watch but don't speak, and I can feel them cataloging every detail. And I know exactly what they see.

They see my mother.

Everyone in this town does. She's loud when she drinks, and she always drinks. She falls in and out of bars and men's beds with the same careless grace she once used on stage in the high school musicals she never quite recovered from.

She used to be beautiful. Now she's just a warning. A whispered "poor thing" at the grocery store. A snicker behind a hand. The kind of woman who forgets to show up to parent-teacher conferences but always remembers karaoke night at the bar.

And me?

I'm the one left picking up the bottles and cooking the eggs and dodging the guys who hang around too long in the kitchen.

People look at me and see what they expect to see. A girl with too much curve and not enough shame. The kind who'll follow in her mother's footsteps because how could I not?

They don't see the straight A's. Or how hard I work to disappear. Or how I never let a boy kiss me—*not once*—because I don't want to give them one more thing to talk about.

They don't see me. Just her.

Lee gestures to the chair across from him, and I sink into it gratefully. My legs feel like jelly, and I'm not sure how much longer they would have held me up.

"Let me see your feet," he says, slapping a hand on his thigh.

"My feet are fine—"

"Kya." The way he says my name brooks no argument. "Let me see."

Before I can protest further, he sighs, sliding off the couch to sit in front of me. I open my mouth to argue but stop when his warm hands wrap around my ankles to place them carefully onto his lap. I wince as he examines the cuts and scrapes, his callused fingers surprisingly tender as they probe the worst of the damage.

"Jesus," he mutters, looking up at one of the other men. "Duck, can you get the first-aid kit?"

"Sure, where is it?" Duck replies, already moving.

"Kitchen. Top cabinet above the fridge."

Lee's touch is impossibly gentle as he examines my torn feet. Duck hands him the kit and a bowl of warm water. Lee gently cleans the cuts, his thumb stroking soothingly along the arch of my foot when I flinch. The antiseptic stings, but his murmured reassurances and the careful way he dabs at each wound make the pain bearable.

"Nearly done," he murmurs before applying the ointment.

When he wraps the bandages around my feet, his movements are precise and sure, as if he's done this more than a few times. Which, considering his position in a Motorcycle Club, and his service history, I guess he might well have.

"Better?" he asks when he's finished, his hands still cradling my bandaged feet.

I can barely speak past the lump in my throat. When was the last time someone took care of me?

"Thank you," I whisper.

He nods once, then looks up at me with those piercing green eyes. "Now. Tell me what happened."

I open my mouth, but the words stick in my throat. How do I tell Lee Armstrong—Emma's brother, the man I used to have such an embarrassing crush on—that my own mother's boyfriend tried to beat me?

"It's okay," he says, and his voice is gentler now. "You're safe here."

I stare at my hands, twisted together in my lap. "My mom was passed out," I whisper. "Again."

"And?"

"And her new boyfriend came over. Rick." The name tastes bitter in my mouth. "He's been staying with us for a few weeks now, and he... he looks at me sometimes. Says things."

Lee goes very still. "What kind of things?"

Heat floods my cheeks. "Just... comments. About how I'm useless. A drain on them. Tonight he..." I swallow hard, forcing the words out. "He cornered me in the kitchen. He was drunk and—" I cut myself off, shaking my head violently.

One of the other men curses under his breath. Someone else mutters something I can't quite catch, but it sounds angry.

Lee's jaw is tight when I finally look up at him. "He hurt you."

Just the one slap, but it was enough.

"I got away," I say, avoiding his question. "I kneed him and ran. I didn't know where else to go. Emma's gone, and I don't have any other friends, and I just... I remembered this place."

Lee reaches out to catch my chin with his hand, turning my head to the left. I close my eyes, knowing he'll see the handprint and slight bruise marked there.

"You did the right thing coming here." His voice is controlled, but there's a cold and dangerous bite lurking underneath. It makes my pulse quicken. "You'll sleep in Emma's room tonight."

It's not a request.

He lets me go, and I nod, suddenly exhausted. The adrenaline is wearing off, leaving behind a bone-deep weariness.

"Go to bed, Kya." Lee says, his voice softer. "Get some rest."

I stand on shaking legs, Lee's clothes swallowing me. "Thank you," I whisper. "For helping me. For not... for not turning me away."

A strange look flickers across his face. "Kya," he says, and my name sounds different in his mouth now. Careful. Important. "You never have to thank me for keeping you safe. Ever."

The weight of his words settles over me like a blanket, and I have to blink back sudden tears. When was the last time someone said something like that to me? When was the last time someone looked at me like I mattered?

I turn, making my way back up the stairs before I do something stupid like cry.

Emma's room is exactly as she left it before she moved to New York. The walls are still painted pale pink, with dance posters covering nearly every surface. Her desk is cluttered with old schoolbooks and jewelry, a thin layer of dust coating everything like snow.

It's a time capsule to a girl who's now living her dream as a principal ballerina with the National Dance Academy.

I crawl into her twin bed, pulling her lavender comforter up to my chin. I close my eyes and try to pretend, just for a moment, that she's still here. That we're still those innocent girls who believed in forever friendships and happy endings.

But then I hear the front door slam, followed by the rumble of motorcycle engines roaring to life. Multiple bikes, from the sound of it. I slip out of bed and tiptoe to the window, pushing aside the sheer curtains just enough to peek out.

Lee strides across the front yard toward his bike, three other men flanking him. Another two men are already on their bikes, waiting.

Even in the dim streetlight, I can see the tension in Lee's shoulders, the way his hands are clenched into fists. He swings a leg over his Harley and kicks it to life, the engine's growl echoing through the quiet neighborhood. Before he can pull away, his gaze lifts to Emma's bedroom window.

My heart skips as our eyes meet across the darkness. His expression is serious, lethal, filled with a promise I don't fully understand but feel in my bones. Even from this distance, I can see the controlled fury radiating from him, the deadly intent written in every line of his posture.

I don't know for certain that he can see me until he jerks his chin up, offering me a half-smile. Then he revs the engine once more and disappears into the night with the others, leaving me standing at the window with my heart hammering against my ribs.

They disappear into the night, and I know—somehow, I know—exactly where they're going.

I should feel guilty. I should be worried about what they might do to Rick, what kind of trouble this could cause. But all I feel is a strange, warm satisfaction in my chest. Someone cares enough to do something. Someone thinks I'm worth protecting.

Time moves strangely after that. I drift in and out of a restless doze, my mind churning with everything that's happened. Every time I close my eyes, I see Rick's face, feel the sharp crack of his hand on my face. But then Lee's voice is there, soothing steady and sure.

You're safe.

I'm not sure how long they're gone, but I jolt awake when I hear the front door open again. I listen to heavy footsteps on the stairs, knowing it's Lee. I slip out of bed and crack open Emma's door, peering into the hallway.

Lee stands at his bedroom door, his back to me. His cut is gone, replaced by a simple black T-shirt that clings to the broad expanse of his shoulders. But it's his hands that catch my attention—his knuckles are raw and swollen, streaked with blood that looks dark in the dim light.

He must sense me watching because he turns, and our eyes meet across the hallway. For a moment, neither of us speaks. The coldness in his expression should scare me, but it doesn't.

"Is he gone?"

Lee nods once. "You're now club property, Kya. You're under the protection of Stoneheart MC."

"What does that mean?" I whisper.

His smile is sharp, all teeth and shadows. "It means you'll never be unsafe again, Kya. Anyone who even thinks about hurting you will have to answer to us. To me."

A voice calls softly from behind him—feminine, sleepy. "Babe? You coming to bed?"

A woman appears in his doorway, barefoot and wearing nothing but one of his T-shirts. She's beautiful in that effortless way some women are, with long blonde hair and legs that go on for miles. She exactly the kind of woman I'd expect him to have in his bed.

The sight of her hits me harder than it should. Of course he has a girlfriend. Of course someone like Lee wouldn't be alone. I'm such an idiot for even—

"Hey, sweetheart," the woman says, noticing me. Her smile is warm, genuine. "You okay? That bruise looks nasty."

I nod, suddenly aware of how I must look in Lee's oversized clothes, my hair probably sticking up at odd angles. "Fine," I mutter, glancing away. "Just tired."

She makes a noise of sympathy. "Get some rest, okay?"

Lee's eyes never leave mine. "Night, Kya."

Then he steps into his room, and the door clicks shut behind him, leaving me alone in the hallway with the memory of his bloody knuckles.

I slip back into Emma's bed and pull the covers over my head, pressing my face into the pillow. I should feel satisfied. After all, I'm safe. And I do, mostly.

But there's something else, too—a hollow ache in my chest

that I'm afraid to name. I fall asleep thinking about green eyes and bruised hands.

I dream of motorcycles and leather cuts, of strong arms and bloody knuckles. I dream of a man who would burn the world down just to keep me safe.

And when I wake, I know what I have to do.

1

KYA

Ten years later

"You know, by my late-twenties, I assumed I'd have my shit together," I mutter, squinting at the trailer I once prayed to escape. "Not be jumping back into this toxic waste dump of a mess."

Instead, I'm standing ankle-deep in patchy gravel, dressed in funeral black, staring at the ghosts of my childhood. The March air cuts through my thick designer coat—the one and only designer thing I owned. I'd bought it to prove I'd made it out.

Fat lot of good it's doing me now.

The place hasn't changed. The trailer still leans to the left like it's nursing a perpetual hangover, and still smells like stale smoke and regret, even from out here. The wind whistles through the busted screen door, and I swear I can hear Mom's voice, scratchy from too many cigarettes and not enough apologies.

Well, look who finally came home.

The irony isn't lost on me. All those years I spent running from this place, building a life that was the exact opposite of everything it represented. Clean lines, neutral colors, a carefully curated existence where everything had its place and nothing reminded me of where I came from. And here I am, right back where I started.

Only now it's mine whether I want it or not.

My mother—Patricia "Patty" Sullivan, serial heartbreaker and occasional karaoke queen—died in a car crash last Tuesday. I got the call from some bored state trooper who couldn't even pronounce my name right, stumbling over the syllables like they were broken glass in his mouth.

"Kee-ah Sullivan?"

"Ky-ah," I'd corrected.

"Kikah?"

"Ky-ah."

"Right, well, I'm sorry to inform you, Ms. Sullivan, your mother has died."

Sadly, it wasn't grief or shock that hit me—it was a hollow recognition that I'd been preparing for this call for years. Mom had been slowly killing herself with alcohol and bad choices since before I could remember. Part of me was surprised it had taken this long. Hearing the news felt a little like hearing the final bell of a fight that had been over long before the referee counted to ten.

The rest of his words became a blur after that until he'd told me something that had brought reality crashing back into focus.

"She had just cashed a check," he'd added casually, like it was an afterthought. "From the state lottery. A million."

I'd laughed. Like, full-body, are-you-kidding-me hysterical laughter that probably made the poor guy think grief had cracked me completely. Of course she won the lottery. Of course she died before spending a cent. And of course she left it all to me.

Even dead, Mom was still capable of turning my life upside down. At least this time it was in a way that might help.

I sigh and drag my suitcase up the steps, the wheels thunking hard against the warped wood. The sound echoes across the trailer park like gunshots, and I half expect Mrs. Kowalski from next door to poke her head out and start asking questions I'm not ready to answer. But the park is quiet, most people already settled in for the evening with their TV dinners and beer and their denial that this is where dreams come to die.

I don't plan on staying long. Just long enough to deal with the estate, sell what I can't stomach keeping, and figure out what the hell to do with a million dollars that feels more like blood money than a blessing.

I fish the key from my bag and unlock the door.

The second I crack it open, the smell hits me.

Rot. Mildew. Garbage.

I gag, slapping a hand over my mouth as I push the door open wider with my foot. The air inside is thick, humid, and foul, like trash left out in the sun to fester. The scent wraps around me like a clawed hand, yanking me straight back to every awful night I spent in this place.

The carpet is stained. The dishes are still in the sink. There's a half-eaten container of Chinese food on the coffee table, furred over in green mold. And the worst part? It's not even surprising.

I stumble back onto the porch, gulping down the fresh air. My eyes sting. My stomach churns.

"Thanks, Mom." I mutter, praying I won't vomit.

When the nausea passes, I lock up the trailer, toss my bag back in my car and do the only rational thing.

I go in search of a drink.

Our small town has two bars—the country club on the far side of town, and Devil's. The country club is member invite only, which leaves me with the only dive bar in fifty miles.

I pull into the parking lot, shaking my head as I park. It seems some things don't change.

The sign still flickers with the word "Bar" in letters that have seen better decades. There's still a dent in the left wall from where Tommy Hendrix crashed his motorcycle into it senior year.

I sit in the car for a moment, hands gripping the steering wheel, trying to work up the courage to walk through those doors. This is where Mom spent most of her evenings for the past thirty years, perched on a barstool, holding court with whoever would listen to her stories about the good old days when she was homecoming queen and the world was full of possibilities.

It's also where I spent some of the longest nights of my childhood, waiting in the car for Mom to stagger out and drive us drunkenly home. It's where I learned to swallow my pride and my shame in equal measure, to smile politely while helping my stumbling, slurring mother to the car as half the town watched, and the other half judged from afar.

But it's the only place that feels right tonight. The only place where I can properly grieve someone who broke my heart long before she was gone.

I push open the door, and it sticks the way it always has, scraping against the frame with a sound like fingernails on a chalkboard. The smell hits me immediately—beer and grease from whatever passes for food in the kitchen, mixed with industrial-strength cleaner and the faint sweetness of spilled whiskey.

It's like stepping into a time capsule, every detail exactly as I remember. The same jukebox in the corner plays some mournful country song about lost love and second chances. The same dartboard hangs slightly crooked on the far wall, just far enough from the pool table that no one would be injured. The same collection of neon beer signs casting everything in shades of red and blue, like the whole place is perpetually bathed in the glow of a police siren.

I don't expect to see Devil—the man, the myth, the leather-wrapped institution himself—behind the bar. He's older now, grayer, the lines around his eyes deeper and more pronounced. But he's still built like a man who bench-presses monster trucks for fun.

When he looks up and sees me, a million emotions flickering across his face. Surprise, maybe, or recognition? But his expression settles quickly into that neutral mask I remember, the one that never gave away what he was thinking.

"Well, well," he drawls, setting down the glass he was polishing. "Look what the cat dragged in."

"Hey, Devil," I say, sliding onto the barstool I used to sneak onto when my mom wasn't looking. The vinyl is cracked in the same places, held together with duct tape that's gone gray with age. "Hit me with something strong."

He raises an eyebrow.

"Rough day?" he asks, reaching for a bottle of whiskey. The good stuff, not the rotgut he used to pour for my mother.

Guess he knows a designer coat when he sees one.

"Rough week. Rough year. Rough fucking decade, if I'm being honest."

He pours without comment, sliding the glass across the bar with practiced ease. When the whiskey hits my throat, I close my eyes and let it burn.

"I heard about your mom," he says quietly. "I'm sorry, kid."

The word *kid* hits me harder than it should. That's what he used to call me back then, when I was ten and thirteen, and seventeen, coming to collect my mother from whatever mess she'd gotten herself into.

I nod, not trusting my voice.

The silence stretches, while around us, the bar continues its eternal rhythm—the murmur of conversation, the crack of pool balls, the distant hum of the air conditioning that's been on its last legs since the Clinton administration.

"You remember that night," I say finally, "when I was sixteen? It was pouring rain, and you called to say Mom was ready to come home."

Devil's hands never stop moving, polishing glasses with the kind of muscle memory that comes from thirty years behind the same bar. But I see the slight pause, the way his shoulders tense just a fraction.

"Which night? There were a lot of them."

"The night she'd been here since noon, and when I got here, she was passed out in the back booth. You were sitting with her, just... watching over her. Making sure nobody bothered her while she slept it off."

His eyes meet mine briefly before returning to his work. "I remember."

"You helped me get her to the car. She was dead weight, but you acted like it was nothing. Like it was just another Tuesday night." I take another sip, smaller this time, letting the whiskey warm me from the inside out. "You could have just let her walk herself home. Could have looked the other way. But you didn't."

"Wouldn't have been right."

"No," I agree. "But not everyone cared about what was right."

Devil sets down the glass he's been polishing and really looks at me for the first time since I walked in. His eyes are the same piercing blue I remember, the kind that seem to see straight through whatever mask you're wearing to the truth underneath.

"Your mom was good people, Kya," he says slowly. "She was fighting demons bigger than herself, but underneath all that pain, she was good people. And you?" His voice gets even gentler, almost fond. "You were just a kid trying to take care of someone who should have been taking care of you."

The words hit me like a sucker punch, unexpected and devastating. I have to look away, blinking back the sudden sting of tears. In all the years since I left this place, no one has ever acknowledged what those nights cost me. No one has ever recognized the weight I carried, the responsibility that should never have been mine.

"She left me everything," I whisper, my voice barely audible over the jukebox. "The trailer, all her debts, and apparently a million dollars from a lottery ticket."

"Yeah, I heard about that." Devil leans against the bar, crossing his arms. "Hell of a thing."

"Is it, though?" I laugh, but there's no humor in it. "She finally got everything she always wanted—enough money to start over, to be somebody new. And she died before she could spend a dime of it."

"Maybe," Devil says carefully, "it wasn't meant for her."

I look up at him sharply. "What do you mean?"

"Maybe the money was for you. Universe moves in mysterious ways."

I snort, swirling my drink. "Yeah. Real mysterious."

We sit in comfortable silence for a moment, both lost in our own thoughts. The bar has gotten busier while we've been talking—a few construction workers settling in at a corner table, some women my age sharing a pitcher and catching up on gossip. Normal Tuesday night stuff, the kind of ordinary human connection I realize I've been missing in my carefully curated Portland life.

"What's your plan?" Devil asks eventually. "You sticking around, or just here long enough to tie up loose ends?"

"Not sure. I'm between jobs right now."

I flip houses. Buy them cheap, fix them up, sell them to people with more money than taste. Turns out I've got a knack for breathing life back into things people think are ruined.

Not sure what that says about me, but I'm sure a therapist could make a pretty penny analyzing it.

Something shifts in Devil's expression, becomes more thoughtful. He reaches for another glass, polishing it with the same methodical precision, but I can practically see the wheels turning in his head.

"A million gives you a nice cushion to take some time off," he says, setting down the glass and really looking at me. "Gives you time to figure out what you want to do with the rest of your life."

"What are you getting at, Devil?"

He's quiet for a long moment, his eyes taking in the bar around us, the scarred wooden floors, the mismatched furniture, the neon signs that have welcomed the lost and lonely for decades. When he speaks, his voice is almost hesitant.

"I've been thinking about retiring, Kya. Thirty years I've been behind this bar, and I'm tired. My joints ache when it rains, and it rains a lot more than it used to. Been thinking it might be time to hand the keys over to someone younger."

My heart skips a beat. "You're selling the bar?"

"Thinking about it. Problem is, this place..." He gestures around the room, taking in the peeling paint and the cigarette-stained walls and the general air of beautiful decay. "It's not just a business. It's a lifeline for a lot of people. Your mom included."

I remain silent at that comment.

"It needs someone who understands that this place is about connection. Someone who won't just rip it apart and slap on some laminate flooring and a rustic fucking beer sign from some trashy website."

I tilt my head. "Are you... warning me off?"

"Nope." He meets my eyes. "I'm offering it to you."

My heart stutters.

"You want *me* to take over Devil's?"

He shrugs. "You flip houses. I've seen your work. You've got a good eye. Clean lines, strong bones. This place? It's got the bones. It just needs someone to see past the nicotine stains and ghosts."

I blink. "You've seen my work?"

"'Course. Your mom showed me."

I file that tidbit away for future Kya's consideration. I'm too raw right now to give it any sort of attention.

I look around at the bar. The worn floorboards. The dim lights. The jukebox that still somehow plays even when no one's touched it in hours.

"You want me to flip your bar?"

"I want you to run it for six months. Clean it up, fix what's broken, figure out if you want to keep it or flip it and go. I'll hand you the keys right now, no cost—just sweat equity and time. After six months, if you want to buy it, I'll give you a price no one else will match. If not, you walk and when I sell, you get a cut of the profit."

It's a business deal. A *good* one.

He leans forward, bracing his hands on the bar. "Come on, you've got time to kill and a million dollars burning a hole in your pocket. What else you gonna do?"

I look around the bar again, trying to see it through different eyes. The worn wooden floors that have absorbed a thousand stories. The chairs where people have shared their deepest secrets and wildest dreams.

It's not glamorous. It's not safe. It's certainly not the life I planned when I was building in Portland.

But maybe that's exactly the point.

"The town won't like it," I say finally. "Patty Sullivan's

daughter taking over Devil's Bar? They'll have plenty to say about that."

Devil's grin is sharp, all teeth and mischief. "Let them talk, sweetheart. You've got something they don't."

"What's that?"

"Money. Power. And most importantly?" His eyes glitter with something that might be pride. "They'll respect you, if you give them the chance."

I drain my whiskey and set the glass down with a decisive clink.

It's insane. Absolutely, completely insane. I should get in my rental car right now, drive to the nearest hotel, and spend the next six months figuring out how to invest a million dollars in something sensible. Index funds, maybe. Real estate in a town that isn't dying. Something safe and boring and guaranteed to increase in value.

Instead, I hear myself saying, "Alright. I'll do it."

Devil's smile could power the neon signs for a week. "I knew you would."

"Don't make me regret this," I warn, but I'm smiling too.

Please, God, don't let this be a stupid mistake.

"Wouldn't dream of it, sweetheart." He extends his hand across the bar, callused and warm and steady. "Welcome home."

I shake it, thinking of how the town will react when they hear the news.

Let the town gossip. Let them whisper about Patty Sullivan's daughter and her grand delusions.

Kya Sullivan is back, and this time I'm not leaving.

Devil holds up the bottle. "Another?"

I push my glass toward him. "Why not?"

2

LEE

The first thing I notice is that the sign's finally fixed.

The "B" in Bar used to flicker like a dying firefly, annoying as hell every time I rode past. But now it glows steady and sharp against the dusk. Strange.

The second thing I notice? The music.

It's not the usual honky-tonk bullshit or the same classic rock that's been on rotation since before I was born. This is something bluesy and low, with a woman's voice thick like honey and heartbreak.

I push through the door and step into the warm, familiar buzz of the bar. Only it feels different somehow. Cleaner, maybe. Like someone's been paying attention to details that've been ignored for years.

I don't come in here as often as I used to—club business has been keeping me busy lately. But tonight I've got a reason. Devil called earlier, said he was finalizing the handover, wanted to give me a heads-up before word got around. As enforcer, it's my job to know who's operating in our territory.

He didn't say who the new owner was, which was weird in itself. Devil's not usually one for mysteries. If anything, he's too direct for most people's comfort. It's what I like most about him.

I spot the old bastard behind the bar, polishing a glass. He's built like a brick shithouse, with the cholesterol to match. The man's a walking heart attack in a leather vest who should've retired five years ago.

"Thought you were hanging up your apron," I say as I approach, sliding onto a barstool that's seen better decades.

He grunts without looking up.

I lean forward, waiting. Within a few seconds a beer appears before me. Devil might not be the most talkative guy, but he knows that's not why we come here.

I take a sip, waiting for him to share. He ignores me, racking glasses and cleaning down counters that are older than sin.

Finally, knowing the stubborn prick is gonna make me ask, I do so.

"Heard you're selling up."

He gives me a look that would make Medusa proud. "I'm finalizing the transition. Handover's done. Place has a new owner as of yesterday."

"You gonna tell me who?" I lean back, studying his face for tells. "Is it someone local? Someone who understands how things work around here?"

He shrugs. "Don't need to. You'll figure it out soon enough."

I narrow my eyes. "Devil, if this is someone who's gonna cause problems—"

"Relax, Harley." The use of my real name makes me sit up straighter. "New owner's not gonna be trouble for the club. If anything, might solve some old problems."

Before I can ask what the hell that's supposed to mean, the bastard walks off, leaving me with more questions than answers. Typical.

Whatever. I've got eyes. I'll work it out.

I drift toward the pool tables, scanning the room. The place looks good—better than it has in years. Someone's replaced the burned-out bulbs, wiped down surfaces that probably haven't seen a clean rag since they were first installed.

Then I see her.

She's bent over, tugging something from under one of the booths, and *fuck me* if this isn't the best view I've had all damn week.

Thick, round hips hugged tight in a pair of light-wash jeans that fit like sin. Thighs for days. The kind of ass that makes a man want to say thank you to the universe, buy her a drink, and then get on his knees just for the honor of worshipping it.

She's soft in all the right places, the kind of woman built to be held. This woman's full-bodied. Lush. Fucking breathtaking.

Her blonde hair's up in a messy bun, little wisps curling down her neck, and she's humming—actually humming—

as she squirms further onto the booth seat, reaching under the table for something.

The sway of her hips, the way her shirt stretches across her back, the peek of skin above her waistband when she shifts...

Yeah. That's a problem.

A very *hot* problem.

She makes a sound of triumph and pushes up, straightening from the booth with an empty bottle in her hand. It's only then, as she turns toward the bar, that my brain slams the emergency brake hard enough to cause whiplash.

Because I know her face.

Even years later, with fuller cheeks and a confidence she didn't used to wear, I know exactly who she is.

"Kya?"

Her name comes out strangled, like it's been scraped over gravel. Like I haven't said it in years, which I haven't. Because why would I? She was Emma's annoying little friend who used to follow us around like a lost puppy.

She was Emma's friend.

She was a kid.

Kya freezes, her head whipping toward me, and I watch as her eyes go wide. For a second neither of us moves. The jukebox keeps playing, but everything else falls away.

This is not the same girl who used to hide behind Emma when I walked into a room. This is not the girl with the too-big eyes and the defensive walls who always looked like she was ready to bolt at the first sign of trouble.

No.

This is a woman.

And not just any woman.

She's all soft curves and unapologetic presence. And my brain—my traitorous, apparently malfunctioning brain—is noticing things about Emma's best friend that I have no fucking business noticing.

Like her full hips and round belly that she doesn't even pretend to hide. She has thighs that look like they could crush a man's ego. And maybe his skull. And fuck if I don't want her to try.

Her shirt stretches over full, heavy breasts in a way that should be illegal. No bra lines I can see, which only makes it worse. *Or better*. Her waist dips in, soft but strong, flaring out to hips made to hold a man's hands.

Her skin has a warm glow to it, like she's finally getting enough sleep or sun. Her cheekbones are a little sharper now, her jaw more defined. There's a faint freckle near her lip I don't remember, and a tiny scar above her brow. But her eyes? They're still that same deep, soul-melting shade of hazel, only now there's *steel* behind them.

Kya stands tall, chin lifted, shoulders relaxed like she finally fits inside her own body. She's not hiding anymore. That's what hits me most—her confidence and calm. The shrinking teen who knocked on my door in the middle of the night is gone, replaced by a woman who knows what she wants and isn't afraid to take it.

And fuck me, if that isn't the biggest fucking turn-on.

What the hell is wrong with me?

"Lee?" Her voice is different too, and hearing my name come from between those lips does something to me that it absolutely should not do.

I clear my throat, trying to get my head back in the game. "You're back."

"I'm back." She sets the bottle down carefully on a table.

"For good?"

"For now." She crosses her arms, and I force myself to look at her face instead of... other things.

"Emma know you're here?"

Something flickers across her face—hurt, maybe, or disappointment. "Not yet."

The silence stretches between us, and I realize I'm staring. Again. At Emma's friend. At someone I used to think of as practically a little sister.

Someone who definitely doesn't look like a little sister anymore.

Get it together, dickhead.

"So," I say, grasping for normal conversation. "This is your place now."

"I guess it is." There's a note of challenge in her voice, like she's daring me to make something of it.

"Since when?"

"Since yesterday." She starts wiping down the bar, movements precise and controlled. "Devil didn't mention that when he called the club?"

That's the thing about Kya, she understands how integrated the club is with this place—with the whole town, really.

"He mentioned the sale. He didn't mention..." I gesture vaguely. "You."

"Well," she says, voice carefully neutral. "Surprise."

I stiffen. *That's one word for it.*

Then it hits me like a physical blow. But it's not just attraction that has my hands clenching into fists. If Kya's here, if she's running Devil's, then she's directly in Summit's crosshairs. And Devil, the manipulative old bastard, put her there.

"Devil!" I bark, scanning the room for him.

The old man emerges from the back hallway, and the guilty look on his face tells me everything I need to know.

"Outside. Now."

"Lee—" Kya starts, straightening up, but I'm already stalking toward the back exit.

Devil follows, and the moment we're in the alley, I round on him.

"What the fuck were you thinking?" I slam him against the brick wall, not hard enough to hurt but enough to make my point. "You sold her the bar? You put a target on her back?"

"Get your hands off me, boy." His voice is calm, but there's steel underneath.

I release him but don't step back. "Summit's been circling this place for months. You know what they're capable of. And you just hand it over to—"

"To family," Devil interrupts. "That girl's been family since she was knee-high, coming in here to collect her mother. She's got more right to this place than anyone."

"She's got no idea what she's walking into!"

"Doesn't she?" Devil straightens his jacket. "Kya Sullivan's tougher than you think. Always has been. She survived Patty, survived this town's judgment, survived on her own for years. She can handle this."

"Not Summit. Not the cartel—"

"With the club's protection, she can." His eyes narrow. "Unless you're saying the MC can't protect its own?"

The accusation hangs between us.

"Besides," Devil continues, "she's exactly what this place needs. What this town needs. Someone who won't roll over for Summit's money."

"You should have told me. We could have found another buyer—"

"There was no other buyer who'd keep it as Devil's. Who'd fight for it." He steps closer. "That girl came back here for a reason, Lee. Maybe you should figure out what that reason is instead of trying to beat me for making a decision."

I turn to find Kya standing in the doorway, arms crossed, eyes blazing.

"If you two are done discussing me like I'm not capable of making my own decisions, I have a bar to run."

The anger in her voice cuts through my protective rage. *Shit.* This isn't how I wanted this to go.

"Kya—"

"No." She holds up a hand. "I get it. Your first instinct when you see me is to be pissed I'm here. Message received."

"That's not—"

"I've got customers."

She disappears inside, leaving me standing in the alley with Devil's knowing look burning into my back.

"Fix it," he says simply, then heads back inside.

I run my hands through my hair, frustrated. She doesn't understand. How could she? She doesn't know about the threats, the missing people, the real danger Summit poses.

When I finally go back inside, she's behind the bar, purposely not looking at me. The hurt in her posture is obvious, and I hate that I put it there.

"Kya."

"What can I get you?" Her tone is professionally cold.

I blow our a breath. "I'm sorry for being an ass. That's not about you. It's about Devil being an ass. Can we start over?"

She arches an eyebrow, staying silent.

I pull a fifty out of my wallet and stuff it in the tip jar. "How about now?"

She stares at me for a beat, a reluctant smile pulling at her lips. "Maybe. What do you want to drink?"

"Just give me a bottle of whatever your most expensive beer is."

"Good choice. Money makes forgiving you a little easier." She reaches down and pulls a foreign beer from one of the fridges, popping the lid before sliding it across the bar.

"Let me start again. How long you been back in town?" I ask, because I need to know how long I've been oblivious to the fact that Emma's little friend grew up into... this.

"About a week."

A week. She's been here a week, and this is the first I'm hearing about it. In a town this size, that's practically impossible unless someone's been deliberately keeping it quiet.

"My mom died," she says suddenly, like she can read the question in my eyes. "Car accident. I had to come back to deal with things."

The words hit me like a physical blow. "Shit. Kya, I'm sorry. I didn't know."

"There's no reason you would have." She shrugs, but there's pain hiding behind the casual gesture. "She left me some money. And this opportunity came up."

"So you decided to buy a bar?"

"It's a good opportunity. Devil made me an offer, and... here we are."

Here we are, indeed. Emma's best friend is back, she owns the bar, and I spent five minutes checking out her ass like some kind of pervert. This day just keeps getting better.

I glance over my shoulder to see Devil lurking in the hall. The bastard. He knows how in the shit the town is right now and he still decided to sell to Kya.

A muscle leaps in my jaw as I turn back to her. I'll be having further words with him later.

Before I can figure out what to say to that, the door opens and Cash walks in, followed by Mack and Bones. They're laughing about something and bringing the cold night air with them. Their voices carry across the room, and I see Kya tense slightly, her eyes tracking their movement.

They haven't noticed me yet, but they will soon enough. And when they do, they're going to want introductions to the new owner. They're going to look at her the way I just looked at her, and for some reason that makes something dark and possessive twist in my gut.

Which is fucked up on about seventeen different levels.

"I should go," I say, straightening.

"You don't have to—"

"Yeah, I do." I drop a twenty on the bar, way too much for one beer, but my hands are apparently not taking orders from my brain right now.

She nods like she understands, but how could she? She doesn't know about club business, or about the careful lines I have to walk as enforcer. She doesn't know that I'm supposed to be the one who keeps everyone in line, not the one who gets thrown off balance by seeing an old friend.

An old friend who looks nothing like the girl I used to know. Now? She's back, grown up, and way too sexy for my peace of mind. And, if I'm honest, a friend who's definitely going to be starring in my X-rated fantasies.

"Lee." My name stops me halfway to the door. When I turn back, she's watching me with an expression I can't read. "It's good to see you."

The words are simple, but they hit me harder than they should. Because despite the confusion, it is good to see her too.

Too good.

"Yeah," I say, my voice rougher than I intended. "You too, kid."

The word *kid* comes out automatically, and the second it's out, I flinch. I hate being called that. Every time someone does, it's like they're erasing everything I'd been through. And even as I say it, I know it doesn't fit. In no way shape or form is Kya a kid. She hasn't been a kid for a long time.

I watch as her expression cools, her smile disappearing. She takes a small step back, and I can feel the apology forming on the tip of my tongue.

Fuck.

I need to get the hell out of here before I do something stupid.

I push through the door and back into the cold night air. I settle on my ride, grateful when the engine roars to life, drowning out the music drifting from the bar and the sound of my own thoughts spinning in circles.

Kya Sullivan is back.

Kya Sullivan owns Devil's Bar.

Kya Sullivan looks like fucking sin.

Don't go there, Armstrong.

I rev the engine and tear out of the parking lot, but I can't outrun the feeling that everything just got a lot more complicated. The careful order I maintain, the rules I enforce, the lines I never cross. It's all suddenly a lot less clear than it was an hour ago.

3

KYA

T he last interview of the day walks through my door at exactly four o'clock, and I already know she's the one.

Mercy Rogers is confident but not cocky, aware but not defensive. She's maybe early thirties, with wild red curls that catch light like copper wire, and intricate sleeve tattoos peeking out from under a crisp white button-down. She's got the kind of curves that fill out her jeans and send men nutty—a woman who takes up space and doesn't apologize for it. Her smile is genuine, reaching green eyes that have obviously seen some shit but haven't lost their sparkle. It's the kind of smile that will definitely get her tips even on bad nights.

She's perfect.

"You're the new owner?" she asks, sliding into the booth across from me without waiting for an invitation.

"Guilty as charged." I close the folder containing the other applications—three college kids who couldn't tell the difference between a Manhattan and a martini, and one guy who kept staring at my chest instead of making eye contact. I shouldn't have to be doing this, but the last bartender, Sarah, quit two days ago for greener pastures in Vegas.

"Tell me why you want to work here."

"Because I need a job, and you need someone who knows the difference between good service and kissing ass." She leans back, completely at ease. "I've been bartending on and off for twelve years. Did five at Murphy's Pub down in Ailington before they closed," she says, referring to a neighboring town. "I freelanced at private events for a while and worked up at the country club for a bit. I'm also a quick study, so within a few shifts, I'll know everyone who walks through that door, what they drink, and which ones tip well."

I like her already.

"Why'd Murphy's close?"

"New owner wanted to turn it into some artisanal craft cocktail place. Charged eighteen dollars for an old-fashioned and wondered why locals stopped coming." She shrugs. "Sometimes people just want a beer and to be left alone, you know?"

Do I ever.

"Why not stay at the country club, I'm sure their pay and conditions are better than I can offer."

Her face turns stoney. "Let's just say they had issues with my...style." She gestures to her tattoos. "Plus, it wasn't a healthy working environment."

"What makes you think this place will be different?"

Mercy glances around, taking in the fresh paint on the walls and repaired stools. "Firstly, it's a biker bar. You're not gonna give me too much grief about the way I look. But it's mostly because you're not trying to change what works. You're just making it better. Dressing it up a bit. I respect that."

Exactly what I was hoping to hear. "You're hired," I say, extending my hand across the table. "Can you start tonight?"

"Hell yes."

After Mercy leaves to grab her gear, I walk through the bar one more time, checking everything. The new chef arrived yesterday and has already transformed the kitchen from a health code violation into something that resembles a functional kitchen. The two regular waitresses are coming in at six, both locals who have worked at Devil's for years and know the clientele. They don't bat an eye at bikers or blue-collar workers wanting to blow off steam.

Devil officially handed over the keys three days ago after onboarding me for two weeks. The old codger clapped me on the shoulder hard enough to dislocate it before walking out the door. If he had a small tear in his eye, you better believe I didn't see it. He's spending his retirement fishing, he said, though I suspect he'll be back to check on the place before the month ends.

A workaholic recognizes another.

The first few days of onboarding were chaos. Inventory hadn't been updated for years, while the books looked like something the CIA might teach in cryptography class. The walk-in freezer held more science experiments than food, and the beer taps seemed to require witchcraft to produce actual beer rather than foam. But underneath all the grime and grease lay good bones. Devil's bar—though Devil himself had only ever called it *The Bar*—had the foundation of a place that could thrive. It just needed someone to give a damn.

So I did.

I started with the basics, deep-cleaning every surface until my fingers were raw. Then I hired a cleaning crew to tackle the bathrooms, because I'd be damned if I was going in there without a hazmat suit, a bull dozer, and a priest on standby. I then reupholstered the booth seating in dark green faux leather—still divey, just less sticky.

A fresh lick of paint turned the walls from grunge into matte charcoal with warm amber sconces to soften the mood. Finally, I sanded and re-stained the bar top, bringing out the old wood grain beneath decades of spilled drinks and cigarette burns.

It's amazing what you can do with some elbow grease, unlimited cash, a severe lack of respect for sleep, and a dogged determination to drown your grief in hard work.

Mrs. Henderson from the diner brought her book club for happy hour this afternoon and pronounced the place "much improved." Coming from her, that's practically a glowing review.

I'm exhausted but satisfied when seven-thirty rolls around and we're steady but not slammed. The regulars have been filtering in, curious about the changes. They ask questions, seemingly waiting for me to turn the place into a wine bar or host yoga brunches.

But then they sit. They drink. They order a meal. And they tell me they'll be coming back tomorrow.

Which has to mean I'm doing something right.

As I fight a yawn, I hear it—the rumble of motorcycles in the parking lot. Multiple bikes, from the sound of it—that distinctive growl that seems to vibrate through your chest whether you want it to or not.

I tense, wondering if Lee is among them, and I hate that my pulse quickens at the possibility. Last night when he walked into my bar, I wasn't prepared for the gut-punch of seeing him again. The boy I'd once harbored an embarrassing crush on has grown into a man who could stop traffic just by breathing. All broad shoulders and controlled danger, he still moves with that same effortless confidence I remember but now it's wrapped in leather and an attitude that makes my mouth go dry.

Goddamn it, Kya. Pull yourself together.

I'd forgotten what it felt like to want someone so badly it physically hurt. The heat that had pooled low in my belly when he looked at me. But then he'd called me "kid," and the spell had shattered, reminding me exactly where I stood in his world. I was, am and forever will be Emma's little friend.

The door opens, and they walk in like they own the place. Which, in a way, I suppose they do. This is their territory, their town, their bar regardless of whose name is on the deed.

The lead guy looks a little like Santa Claus with his beer gut, white hair, ajd gray-white beard. That's Duck, I remember him from the times he visited Lee's dad, Stone, at their house. Behind him are guys I went to school with, Cash and Mack, both looking like the very definition of "dangerous bikers." And bringing up the rear, moving with that same effortless, cocky swagger I remember all too well, is Lee.

I'm not emotionally, mentally or physically prepared to see him again.

Especially not after last night.

I close my eyes, sucking in a breath.

Damn, but my whole body lit up like a struck match. I'd forgotten what that felt like. No, scratch that—I'd never felt that before. The heat low in my belly. The thrum under my skin. The way every nerve ending perked up just because he was breathing the same air. It was a gut-punch of desire that stole every coherent thought I had.

I blink open, watching as he heads my way.

He's broader than he used to be. Thicker in the shoulders. Tighter in the jaw. That leather cut hugs his frame like a second skin, and the dark T-shirt underneath stretches across a chest that movie stars would die to have. His thighs are tree trunks in those worn jeans. His hands—*God, his hands*—hang loose by his sides like he hasn't decided whether to hold you or ruin you.

And don't even get me started on that mouth. That full-lipped, no-nonsense mouth that could probably make a girl forget her own damn name.

My throat goes dry. My nipples tighten against my bra—the traitors. I shift my weight, suddenly hyper-aware of the way my jeans cling to my hips.

My body hasn't gotten the memo that this is a very bad idea. He's trouble with a capital do not touch.

"Evening, boys," Mercy calls out, already reaching for bottles before they've even ordered. "You want a table?"

"That'd be great, darlin'." Duck turns my way, nodding politely. "Kya."

For a split second I think Lee might have mentioned me to him. Afterall, It's been years since I've seen him, and I highly doubt he'd remember the slip of a girl I was once. Then I glance down at the name tag pinned to my shirt and bite back a laugh. Of course he knows my name—it's written right there in bold black letters on a little plastic rectangle.

Silly girl.

Desperate for something to do with my hands, I pick up a cloth and begin drying a glass that doesn't need it. "Welcome. First round's on the house."

Duck's eyebrows rise slightly. "That's generous."

"Good neighbors support each other," I say, meeting his gaze steadily. "The club is always welcome here."

It's a calculated move—establish goodwill early, show respect for their position in the local hierarchy, make it clear I'm not looking for trouble. From the subtle nod Duck gives me, I know he appreciates the gesture.

I risk a glance Lee's way, but he's turned away from me,

watching the players at the pool table. His jaw is tight, shoulders rigid, like he's working very hard to ignore me.

Good. We're on the same page.

They settle at their usual table in the back corner, and I watch Mercy work. She's clearly someone who's served bikers before, friendly but not flirty, respectful but not intimidated. Within minutes, she's got them laughing, and the tension I hadn't even realized I was carrying starts to ease.

The crowd begins to pick up as the Friday night regulars drift in. It's busy and chaotic, but manageable. I find a flow with the waitresses, laughing and joking with them as we trade empties and cash for full glasses of whatever beverage our patrons desire.

I keep an eye on the bikers, but they stay in their back corner, playing pool and shooting the shit. It's an hour or so before one of the younger members separates from the group and approaches the bar.

His cut identifies him as Bones, the tail gunner, and he leans against the bar with an easy grin. He's maybe late twenties, dark hair a little too long, mischief written all over him, and laugh lines that suggest he's more about having a good time than causing trouble.

"Well, well," he says, giving me a slow once-over that somehow manages to feel more curious than sleazy. "So you're the new boss lady. Devil's been pretty tight-lipped about you."

I keep polishing glasses, but I meet his gaze with a smile. "That's me. Kya."

"Bones," he replies, offering his hand across the bar. His handshake is firm but not aggressive. "Gotta say, this place looks good. You've done good work."

"Thanks."

"I'm serious. You've done the impossible. You've made Devil's feel clean. I mean, it's still a dive, but like, a dive with standards."

"High praise," I deadpan, quietly amused by him.

He grins. "Seriously. I've seen a lot of MC bars. Most smell like sweat, beer, and bad decisions. This one smells like... Pine-Sol."

That makes me laugh. "I'll take that as a compliment."

"You should." He leans in just slightly. "If you need help with anything—fixing things, heavy lifting, threatening unsavory customers—I'm your guy. I work for beer and flattery."

"I've got a fridge full of one, and I'm not above the other."

He places a hand over his chest, mock-swooning. "Marry me."

I raise a brow. "You're that easy?"

"Ma'am," he says, grinning, "I'm a biker, of course I'm easy."

That earns another laugh, and for a moment, I forget the weight of grief and pressure and small-town eyes.

It feels... nice.

"What can I get you?"

"Three of whatever is on tap, a cider, and a packet of those pretzels."

"Got it."

I turn to grab a glass, I feel it—that prickle at the back of my neck. The unmistakable weight of someone watching.

I glance up, instinct pulling my eyes toward the far corner of the room.

Lee.

He's seated in the shadows, beer in hand, gaze locked on me. Not angry. Not amused. Just *watching*, his expression utterly unreadable.

My stomach does a slow, traitorous flip.

I turn back to the tap, pretending I didn't see him. Pretending my hands aren't shaking just the tiniest bit as I pour the next beer.

Stop it, Kya!

Bones nudges a coaster across the bar with one finger. "But seriously—grab dinner with me sometime. Low pressure. I promise not to propose unless the food's really good."

Before I can respond, Lee appears beside him as if he materialized out of thin air. "Bones."

"Hey, brother." Bones doesn't move, seemingly unfazed by Lee's sudden appearance. "Just welcoming our new neighbor to the community. You met Kya?"

Lee doesn't even look at him. His eyes are all on me. And suddenly the bar feels a few degrees warmer.

His voice is low. "Yeah, I've met her." Something about the way he says it makes my stomach drop. And flutter.

Bones's brows lift slightly. He looks between us, catching whatever undercurrent just passed through the air. "Right," he says with a slow, easy grin. "There's history here."

I turn away from Lee, smiling at Bones. "I was best friend's with Lee's sister back in school."

"You aren't still?"

I shake my head with a laugh. "We're still friends, but she's gone on to bigger and better things in New York."

"The dancer, right?"

Lee nods once.

"And you?" Bones asks, glancing between us. "With a smokeshow like Kya—you two ever have anything?"

I flush, glancing away as I place the final drink on a tray. "No. Lee was too cool for a dweeb chick like me."

"You weren't a dweeb." Lee's sharp denial surprises me.

"Excuse me?" I gesture to myself. "Dude, I was grade A awkward."

He makes a frustrated sound under his breath. "No, you weren't."

I cross my arms, eyebrows raised. "You do realize I wore knee-length cargo shorts and read *Lord of the Rings* fanfic on my phone during lunch, right?"

His jaw flexes. "And? Reading doesn't make you awkward.

Way I remember it, you were smart and funny. And gorgeous. You always have been."

I freeze.

Oh.

Bones whistles low, dragging his drink toward him like he just scored ringside seats. "Well damn. You two selling tickets to this show, or am I just lucky to be here?"

I snort, trying to break the tension with humor even as my stomach tightens. "Lee's joking," I say, reaching for my dishrag. "He knows he's wrong."

"I'm not."

There's a beat of awkwardness before Bones stands. "Well, it's been nice to meet you, Kya. Offer stands if you change your mind." He claps Lee on the shoulder. "See you back at the table."

Lee makes a noncommittal noise, his gaze locked on me as Bones lifts the tray of drinks with one hand and carries his own glass back to their table.

With Bones gone, tension creeps in. A moment hangs between Lee and I, and I can sense the subtle shift in dynamics. He breaks the silence.

"Sorry about that."

"About what? Bones being polite, charming, and asking me to dinner?" I raise an eyebrow.

"You should be careful. He's a player."

I snort, amused. "And you're not?"

His expression hardens slightly. "I'm looking out for you."

"I don't need looking out for, Lee. I'm not seventeen anymore."

Something flickers across his face at that—memory, maybe, or acknowledgment. "No," he says quietly. "You're definitely not."

Goosebumps rise along my skin, a honey heat uncurling in my belly at his admission.

I want to prod him, ask him why he said it the way he did, but he nods once and heads back to his table, leaving me with the distinct feeling that this conversation is far from over.

After they're both back at their table, Mercy slides over, shaking her head with an amused smile. "Well, that was interesting."

"Part of the job," I say, trying to project calm I don't entirely feel.

"Honey, I've been serving drinks for most of my adult life, and I know a pissing contest when I see it." She glances toward the corner table where Lee is pointedly not looking in our direction. "That man's got some serious feelings brewing."

"It's complicated," I say finally.

"The best ones always are." Mercy grins and heads back to her tables, leaving me alone with my thoughts and the awareness that Lee's presence seems to fill the entire bar, even when he's trying to ignore me.

The rest of the night passes without incident. The MC table stays through last call, their voices low and serious as they discuss whatever club business brought them here. Lee doesn't approach the bar again, but I feel his eyes on me throughout the evening—a steady, watchful presence that should annoy me but instead makes me feel strangely safe.

When they finally leave, Duck stops by the bar to settle their tab. "Good drinks, good service," he says, dropping cash on the bar with a generous tip. "We'll be back."

"You're always welcome here," I tell him, and mean it.

He nods, then leans in slightly, voice dropping to just above a whisper. "Anyone gives you trouble, you call."

My throat goes tight. "Thank you."

He straightens. "Night, Kya."

They file out into the cold night air, engines roaring to life in the parking lot. I watch through the window as they disappear into the darkness, Lee bringing up the rear on his black Harley.

"You okay?" Mercy asks, starting to stack chairs on tables.

"Yeah," I say, though I'm not entirely sure that's true. "Just thinking."

We're adults now. Complicated, damaged adults with histories and baggage and no good reason to be circling each other like this.

I just hope we're both smart enough not to do anything stupid.

4

LEE

My father, our President, raps his knuckles on the table. The room falls silent.

"Let's bring this to order. Church is in session," Stone says, his gaze flinty. Silver threads through his dark hair now, though he's still young and fit at just forty-eight. Since divorcing my mom, he's had club girls all over him but no real relationships. I don't begrudge him that. He could have cheated on her years ago when she first left, but he stayed true until the papers were signed.

He's a good father and an even better President. Our gazes meet across the table, and I can see that he's missed nothing. Not the quiet edge in the air, and certainly not the unease of the members around the table.

Tank, our Vice President, opens with the update we all knew was coming. "Summit's pushin' again. Rezoning surveys went out last week to every resident in the western neighborhoods—Oakridge, Pinecrest, and all along Iron

Way. They're quiet about it, but they're laying the groundwork for a takeover."

Summit Development. That name's been a curse on our town since the first slick brochure showed up in mailboxes. All shining smiles and luxury promises, offering to buy up land for big money, claiming they'd bring jobs, growth, and opportunity to our little patch of dust. For a while, it worked. People sold. Some needed the money. Some didn't know better. But most? They stayed.

Turns out, Summit wasn't interested in community. They wanted control. When the townsfolk didn't take their offers, they started squeezing—buyouts, harassment, property disputes, fines. They'd drag old-timers to court over barely legible land rights, tip off inspectors to code violations, and bury folks in red tape and fines until giving up was easier than fighting.

We mostly put a stop to that a few months back. But now? They're back and they aren't fucking around.

Cash, our Treasurer, taps his fingers restlessly against the table. The guy's a few years younger than me with a face that movie stars would kill to have. We'd give him shit for it if it wasn't for the fact he's the best damned accountant the club has ever had. He's been tracking Summit's finances like a bloodhound.

"They're losing money, fast. They've had six failed buy attempts in the last two months. That's not counting legal delays from the residents we've helped stall. Mrs. Wilson's property alone has cost them nearly fifty grand in legal fees."

"And that makes them dangerous," Duck says, leaning forward. "Corner a wolf and you'd better be ready to bleed."

White-bearded and barrel-chested, Duck's retired these days, but he was Sergeant at Arms before Hawk. He's the kind of man whose words still carry weight when he chooses to speak. There's nods from those around the table.

"Which is why we're taking this seriously," Stone says, glancing at Hawk. "Hawk's found us a contact—Josie Bright. Lawyer. Quiet, effective, not local enough to scare off."

Hawk is already scowling from his seat near the door. Our Sergeant at Arms, the guy is big, and built like a semi with a bad attitude. Hawk's responsible for protecting the club from dangers—internal and external. He enforces the rules, and trust me, you don't want to be on the receiving end when those rules get broken.

Unless you're his kids. In which case, you get a free pass.

"The meet will be at Devil's," he says, and my jaw tightens.

It makes sense—Devil's is neutral ground. We can make it appear as if the lawyer is just getting chatted up by one of the club, not taking a proper meeting. But hosting it there will mean putting Kya in Summit's scope, and I'm not okay with that.

Fuck. This is not where my head needs to be right now.

Bones lifts a brow. "We worried about bugs in the clubhouse?"

Axel shakes his head. "No, but we can't rule out surveillance. Summit might not be listening to us, but they're watching. Devil's got more foot traffic, more noise. Safer to talk there."

"I've got more bad news," Cash says, shaking his head. "They're funding three seats in the local election. And they've pumped big money into those candidates."

"Council elections are next week," Mack, our Secretary, adds. "If Summit gets those seats, they'll have the numbers to push zoning change through. It'll gut the local protections. They'll be able to fast-track demolitions."

"And the residents will be out on their asses," I mutter, thinking of the families I've known my whole life who've lived in those homes for generations.

Stone nods. "Which is why we're getting ahead of this. This lawyer—Josie—she specializes in land protection, council law, and corruption cases. She's gonna tell us what legal recourse we have and whether we've got the legs for a class action."

Hawk grunts. "Or if it's time to stop talking and start punching."

"No one's throwing punches yet," Stone says calmly. "We're smarter than that."

"But ready," Tank adds. "Always ready."

"What about the construction equipment?" I ask, thinking about our previous tactics. "Last time we had some success disabling their bulldozers to delay the work."

Axel nods. "Still on the table. But they've upped security. Got ex-military types patrolling now, not just rent-a-cops."

I lean back in my chair, gaze drifting over the old photos on the wall—rides long past, brothers we've lost. Summit thinks they're dealing with townsfolk. They don't understand that what they're pushing against is blood, bone, and legacy.

They're building condos. We're protecting our people.

And I'll burn their entire empire down before I let them take another inch.

"One more thing," Stone adds, his gaze sweeping the room. "Devil's new owner. Kya Sullivan."

My shoulders tense at her name.

"What about her?" I ask, trying to keep my voice neutral.

"We need to know where she stands," Stone says. "Devil trusted her, but this isn't just about selling beer anymore. If we're using her place for meetings, we need to be sure she's solid."

"She's solid," Duck says firmly. "She knows her place and what she owes the club. Girl's got steel in her spine."

"May be," Stone concedes. "But Summit's got deep pockets. And everyone has a price."

The implication sends a flare of anger through me. "Not her," I say, more sharply than intended. "You know her. She's one of us."

All eyes turn to me, and I realize I've said more than I meant to. Bones raises an eyebrow, a hint of a smirk playing at his lips.

"She was one of us. She's been gone a long time."

My jaw tightens at the unexpected skepticism in my dad's tone. "Like Duck said, she's solid."

"She may be, but until we know for sure, she needs watching," Stone decides. "Lee, that's on you. Keep an eye on her, feel her out on Summit. See where her loyalties lie."

Great. Just what I need—official orders to spend more time around the woman who's already taking up too much space in my head.

Knew I should have stayed in bed today.

"Church dismissed," Stone says, pushing back from the table.

As the others rise, Bones claps a hand on my shoulder. "You good?"

"Always."

He grins, seeing right through me. "Right. So that's why you nearly bit Stone's head off at the suggestion your girl might be bought."

"She's not my girl," I growl.

"If you say so," he laughs, raising his hands in mock surrender. "Course, if she ain't yours, then you won't mind me taking her on a date, right?"

The muscle in my jaw ticks, but I keep my expression carefully neutral. "Knock yourself out."

"Great," Bones grins, clearly enjoying himself. "I'll pick her up Friday night. Take her somewhere nice, show her a good time..."

"Do whatever you want," I say, but my hands clench into fists. Every instinct is screaming at me to tell Bones to back the fuck off, that Kya is off-limits. The thought of another man's hands on her makes me want to commit murder.

Instead, I force a shrug. "Just don't come crying to me when she breaks your heart."

Bones chuckles and heads for the door, leaving me alone with the very real urge to punch something.

The room empties slowly, brothers breaking off into smaller conversations. I stay seated, lost in thought until I realize Stone hasn't moved either. He's watching me with that look —the one that says he's seeing more than I want him to.

"Something on your mind?" I ask when everyone else has cleared out.

He leans back, crossing his arms. "You tell me."

I meet his gaze, knowing there's no point playing dumb. "It's complicated."

"Always is with women," he says with a slight head tilt. "Especially the ones who get under your skin."

"Kya's not..." I start, then stop myself. No point lying to a man who taught me how to lie. "She's not what I expected, coming back. She's different."

An image of Kya flashes in my mind. Not just the curves and confidence, but the steel in her eyes, the way she held her ground. The woman she's become is a far cry from the scared kid who showed up on our doorstep that night in the rain.

Stone studies me for a long moment. "Just remember—club comes first. Always has."

"I know that."

"Do you?" His eyes search mine. "Because I've seen that look before. On Hawk when he met Andi. On Axel with Poppy. It's the look of a man whose priorities are shifting."

"My priorities are fine," I say firmly. "I'll keep an eye on Kya, but I'm not getting involved. She's off-limits."

Stone raises an eyebrow. "Who said anything about getting involved?"

Caught. Damn it.

He stands, clapping a hand on my shoulder. "Just be careful, son. Hearts and club business make for messy combinations."

I don't have to ask how he knows since I witnessed it firsthand.

"Kya's not a problem," I insist, but the words sound hollow even to my ears.

Stone just gives me a look that says he was young once too, and he understands far more than I want him to. "Like I said. Be careful." He hesitates. "But don't be afraid to get close if you need to. The club always comes first."

He leaves me sitting alone in the chapel. Outside, engines roar to life as the brothers head out into the night.

I rub a hand over my face, feeling the weight of the patch on my back. Keeping an eye on Kya is one thing. Keeping my hands to myself might be another problem entirely.

Fuck. This is not what I need right now.

But orders are orders. And Dad's right—club comes first. Always.

5

KYA

My first week as the owner of Devil's officially ends with me flopped on my couch surrounded by crumpled receipts and ledger sheets that make about as much sense as quantum physics. The light from my laptop casts a blue glow across the chaos of my small living room.

I didn't have the stomach to stay in Mom's trailer—not with the smell and memories—so I'd rented a small cottage on the edge of town. It's nothing fancy, just a one-bedroom with creaky floorboards and a temperamental water heater, but it's clean and it's mine. For now, at least.

My phone buzzes, dragging me from the edge of sleep. I blink at the screen, surprised to see Mercy's name.

MERCY

You alive, boss?

KYA

Barely. Why?

MERCY

Need your sign-off on an order. Plus Duck
just called. MC needs a favor.

I frown at the message. A favor? From me?

KYA

Did he say what about?

MERCY

Nope. Just asked if you could call him
ASAP.

KYA

Thanks. Approve the order. I'll give Duck a
call.

I'm about to set the phone down when it rings.

"Hello?"

"Kya." Duck's gravelly voice fills my ear. "Got your number from Devil. You got my message?"

"Yeah. How can I help?"

"We need your backroom for a few hours. And your discretion."

I frown, drawing a pattern in the rug with my big toe. "Is it illegal?"

"No."

"Is it going to get me in trouble with anyone?"

"Not if we can help it."

I close my eyes, sighing heavily. "That doesn't sound good."

"Don't worry about it. This is club business. It's sensitive but there won't be blowback. Promise."

I barely resist sighing once more. "Fine. But I'm charging you double for the room. Consider it danger pay."

He chuckles. "You do that, sweetheart."

The call ends, leaving me staring at my phone with a knot in my stomach. What the hell had I just agreed to? I guess I'd find out tomorrow.

Thursday arrives with steel-gray clouds and a chill that cuts through my jacket as I unlock the front door of Devil's. The bar feels different in the daylight. The scuffs on the floorboards are more visible, the wear on the bar stools more apparent. It's like seeing someone without their makeup on—all their flaws and character laid bare.

It's my favorite part of the day.

I'm restocking the bar when I hear the first rumble of motorcycles in the parking lot. My watch reads 2:45. They're early.

The door opens, and Duck enters first, followed by Stone, Emma and Lee's dad, and the club's president. I haven't seen him in years, but the silver threading through his dark hair suits him.

Behind him comes a steady stream of leather and denim—Cash and Mack, Bones, and several others I recognize from around town but don't know by name. Lee enters with the group and his gaze locks with mine across the room. His expression is unreadable as he takes in the sight of me here, in the middle of club business.

Last to enter is a man with a carefully trimmed beard and piercing eyes that seem to catalogue every detail of the room. His cut identifies him as "Axel - Road Captain."

"Kya." Duck nods in greeting. "Appreciate you letting us use the space."

"My pleasure," I say, gesturing toward the back room where I've already set up tables and chairs. "Coffee's fresh if anyone wants some."

Stone approaches, his eyes warming with recognition. "Kya Sullivan. It's been a while."

"Mr. Armstrong." I extend my hand, expecting a shake. I get a hug instead. A real one, like what I imagine a father might give a daughter he hasn't seen in years.

It's warm and tight, and for a beat I let myself pretend he's my parent, grateful to have me home.

Silly girl. You don't have any family left.

"It's Stone to you now," he says with a slight smile as he puts me back on the ground. "You're not a kid anymore."

"No, sir," I agree. "Not for a long time."

His eyes study me for a moment, something thoughtful in his expression. "Duck tells me you're okay with us hosting this meeting."

"Devil explained this happens occasionally. I understand."

"It does. Though we try to keep the imposition to a minimum." His gaze is piercing when it meets mine. "Just understand that what we discuss here stays here."

"I've always been good at keeping secrets," I tell him, meeting his stare steadily. The unspoken reference to all those nights I spent covering for his daughter, and all the times he'd pretended not to notice me sneaking out of their house at dawn, hangs between us.

His lips twitch as if he's amused. "That you have. Let's get started."

We move to the back room, but before anyone sits, Axel pulls out a small device from his jacket pocket.

"Standard procedure," he explains, seeing my questioning look. "Just checking for bugs."

He sweeps the room methodically, the device making occasional beeps as he passes it over light fixtures, under tables, and around the edges of the room. When he's done, he nods to Stone.

"Clean."

I linger by the door. "Need anything else from me?"

Stone exchanges a glance with Duck, then shakes his head. "We're good, Kya. Thanks."

The dismissal is clear. I nod, backing out of the room and pulling the door closed behind me. I stand there for a moment, listening to the low murmur of voices starting up on the other side.

Part of me knows I should respect their privacy. But another part—the part that grew up in this town, that understands the consequences of ignorance—can't just walk away. Not when it sounds like something big is happening.

I head to the storeroom next door, stepping carefully around boxes of liquor and paper goods. While cleaning this beast of a building, I've begun to leave its the quirks. Which is how I found the small gap in the shared wall where a pipe had once run through. It's been patched on the meeting room side, but if you know where to look, you can still hear through it. Not to mention the small peep hole beside it.

I had no doubt Devil knew all about this—and listened in regularly on anyone using the room. Cheeky bugger.

I press my ear against the wall, straining to make out the voices. That's when I hear it. A woman.

Turning, I peep through the hole and am surprised to see a woman in her early--forties with warm brown skin and natural curls which are pulled back in a neat bun. She's wearing an expensive suit and carrying a sleek leather briefcase.

"You must be Ms. Bright," Lee says, his posture shifting subtly.

"Josie, please. Ms. Bright makes me sound like I'm teaching kindergarten."

"Lee Armstrong," he introduces himself then the others at the table.

She sets her briefcase on the table. "I've reviewed the initial documents you sent. You've got a serious situation on your hands."

"Very," Stone agrees. "Lee was just briefing us on Summit's political moves."

Josie opens her briefcase, pulling out a folder. "That tracks with their MO in other communities. They establish a presence, then use money to push through zoning changes that benefit their projects and harm existing residents."

I frown, pressing closer to the wall. People are being pushed out of their homes? The thought makes my stomach churn with anger. This is my town, my people. How is this not splashed across the front page of the newspaper? And why is the MC involved?

"Can we stop them?" Duck asks.

"That depends on a number of factors," she says, spreading out several documents. "I need to understand what evidence we can gather, how organized the community response is, and whether we can find a legal angle to challenge their operations."

Their voices drop, forcing me to return to the pipe, straining to hear.

"... Summit's changing tactics," Lee says, his voice carrying better than the others. "They've been trying to push residents out by making their lives difficult—cutting utilities, creating code violations, blocking road access. But now they're going legitimate. Or at least, pretending to."

The casual cruelty of it hits me like a physical blow. These aren't just numbers on a development plan—these are real people's lives being destroyed. My anger builds with each detail, and I find myself leaning forward, desperate to hear more.

"What do you mean?" Josie asks.

"They've got three candidates running for city council," Lee explains. "All of whom are positioned as 'concerned citizens' who want to 'revitalize' Stoneheart."

Duck's gravelly voice comes through next. "Revitalize is just code for 'push out the poor folk.'"

"Exactly," Lee agrees. "But it gets worse. We've got sources who say Summit's already greasing palms on the current council. That's why they're getting all their permits pushed through while everyone else is stuck in red tape hell."

I shift, trying to hear better as Axel mentions something about a construction company and someone named Poppy.

"The Bennett Construction situation was just the beginning," Axel says, his tone gruff. "Now they're sending out rezoning questionnaires to residents, making it sound like they're gathering community input, when really they're just identifying which neighborhoods to target next."

The conversations continue, and I can hardly believe what I'm hearing. If the club is correct, that means there's a corrupt organization operating out of our town.

But for what purpose?

I jump as warm breath brushes against the shell of my ear, Lee's voice a low rumble that sends goosebumps racing down my arms.

"Find what you're looking for?"

I spin, startled, and suddenly we're face-to-face, our noses almost touching. My heart hammers against my ribs as I take in his piercing gaze, the way his jaw is set with barely controlled tension. I try to step back but my foot catches on a box of stock behind me, and I stumble.

Lee's hands shoot out, gripping my hips to steady me, his fingers strong and sure against the curve of my waist. My palms flatten against his chest automatically, and I can feel the solid thud of his heart underneath the material of his shirt, beating just as fast as mine.

"I—" I start, but there's no good excuse for being caught with my ear literally to the wall.

"Save it." His voice is low, not angry but not exactly thrilled either. "You want to know what's going on."

I nod, watching him sigh.

"Here's the short version, Summit Development isn't just buying up properties around town. They're funded by cartel money. We believe they're using construction and development as a front to laundering cash and are setting up smuggling routes through the old mining tunnels."

My mouth drops open. "Cartel? As in *drug* cartel?"

He finally lets me go. "Yep," he confirms grimly. "And now they're trying to get their people on the city council to make their operations even easier."

"Holy crap," I mutter. "I had no idea it was that serious."

Lee studies me, his expression grim. "Knowing this information is dangerous, Kya. Listening at walls gives you information you may not want. I'm only telling you this because now that you're running the bar, Summit's goons are likely to zero in on you. You need to be careful."

A chill runs down my spine, but I shake it off.

"I want to help," I say, surprising both of us.

"This isn't your fight, Kya."

"Maybe not," I say, stepping closer. "But it's my town, and whether you like it or not, I'm already in this."

His eyes narrow as he studies me. "You think you can go toe-to-toe with a cartel?"

"No," I admit. "But I know how to listen. I know people. And this place is a watering hole for the whole damn town. That means I hear things. And if I can help you spot patterns, track conversations, flag who's been talking to who? Then yeah, I can go toe-to-toe in my own way."

His expression shifts—just a flicker—but it's there. Respect. Maybe a little exasperation, too.

"You always were stubborn," he mutters.

"You like that about me," I fire back.

That earns me the ghost of a smile.

He jerks his chin toward the back. "Come on then. Might as well hear it from the source instead of through walls."

Heat rises to my cheeks, but I follow him back to the meeting room. The men look up as we enter, a few eyebrows rising at my presence, but Stone just nods as if he expected to see me.

I settle into a chair in the corner, trying to absorb everything as Josie lays out potential approaches from challenging the rezoning questionnaires to investigating campaign finance violations, and even gathering data for a potential RICO charge.

She taps her pen against the table. "Here's what I suggest. First, we establish a legal defense fund for residents facing pressure from Summit. Second, we file public records requests for all communications between Summit and council members. Third, we challenge the rezoning questionnaires as misleading and potentially fraudulent."

"And if that doesn't work?" Axel asks.

Josie meets his gaze steadily. "Then we prepare for a longer fight. Class action suits take time, but they can be effective. Especially if we can prove corruption or criminal activity."

The discussion continues for another hour, detailed and methodical. I'm impressed by Josie's command of the legal landscape and her clear-eyed assessment of what they're up against. She doesn't sugarcoat the challenges, but she also doesn't back down from them.

"I'll take the case," she says finally, gathering her papers. "But I need everything you can get me—financial records, testimony from residents, any evidence of wrongdoing. The more ammunition I have, the better our chances."

Stone nods. "You'll have it. We'll start organizing the community defense fund today."

"Good." She stands, extending her hand to Stone. "I'll be in touch with next steps."

As the meeting breaks up, I slip out to the main bar, needing a moment to process everything I've heard. Summit Development isn't just some faceless corporation trying to gentrify our town, they're a criminal enterprise potentially involved in disappearances, maybe even murders. And now I'm right in the middle of it.

Holy crap, Kya. You really got yourself in deep shit this time.

The sound of footsteps makes me look up to find Lee approaching, his expression thoughtful.

"You okay?" he asks, leaning against the bar across from me.

I nod, though I'm not entirely sure that's true. "Just... processing."

"It's a lot to take in," he acknowledges. "Devil should have read you in before handing over the keys. I doubt this is what you signed up for when you bought the bar."

"No," I agree. "And you can bet your bottom dollar I'll be giving Devil a swift kick to the shin the next time I see him. But this is what's happening, and I'm in it now." I glance up at him, studying the lines of his face. "How long has this been going on?"

"Summit showed up about a year ago," he says. "Started small—buying foreclosed properties, offering to 'revitalize' the downtown area. By the time we realized what they were really up to, they'd already sunk their hooks in deep."

"Jesus," I whisper, sick to my stomach.

Lee watches me carefully. "You sure you want to be involved in this, Kya? It's not too late to walk away. Sell the bar back to Devil, use that lottery money to start over somewhere else."

The question catches me off guard. "How do you know about the money?"

He grins. "Small town, remember?"

I nod slowly, considering his question. Do I want to be involved in this? I came back to Stoneheart to deal with my mother's estate, not to own a bar or get caught up in cartel business.

But then I think about the town. Not just as it is now, but as it was. For all its flaws and painful memories, this place shaped me. And there are good people here who don't deserve to be pushed out or terrorized by some faceless corporation.

"I'm not going anywhere," I say finally. "This is my home too."

He nods once, then starts to speak again when Duck calls his name from across the room.

"Coming," he calls back, then turns to me. "We'll talk more later. Lock up tight tonight. And if anything feels off, anything at all, you call."

"I don't have your number," I point out.

The corner of his mouth twitches. "Check your phone."

He rejoins the others as they file out, Josie already deep in conversation with Stone and Axel about next steps. I watch them leave, one by one, until the bar is empty again. Only then do I pull out my phone to find a text from a new contact.

> **LEE**
>
> Call if you need anything, Kya. I mean it.

I stare at the screen, a complicated mix of emotions swirling in my chest. Despite everything—the danger, the uncertainty, the history between us—something about knowing Lee is watching out for me makes me feel safer than I have in years.

Damn it.

KYA

The lunch rush is finishing when the front door of the bar swings open. Framed against the bright afternoon sunlight stands a man in a tailored suit that probably cost more than my monthly rent. I've been back in Stoneheart long enough to know that well-fitted suits like that don't walk into dive bars like mine unless they want something.

He scans the room, gaze landing on me behind the bar. The smile he offers as he approaches doesn't reach his eyes.

"Afternoon," I say, wiping my hands on a towel. "What can I get you?"

"I'm looking for the owner." His voice is city smooth, and it immediately puts me on edge.

"You found her."

His eyebrows lift slightly with surprise that he quickly masks. "Ms. Sullivan? David Crane." He extends his hand across the bar. "I represent Summit Development. I was hoping we might have a quick chat?"

My stomach knots, but I keep my expression neutral as I shake his hand. "Sure. I've got a few minutes. Would you like a drink?"

"Just water, please."

I slide a glass his way and nod toward the office behind the bar. "Follow me."

As I lead him through, I feel the eyes of the few remaining customers on us. Word travels fast in small towns, and being seen with a Summit suit won't go unnoticed.

My office—which is really just a glorified closet with a desk—isn't much, but it's private. I settle into my chair, gesturing for him to take the one across from me.

"What can I do for Summit Development, Mr. Crane?"

He sets his water down carefully, straightening his already straight tie. "I'll be direct, Ms. Sullivan. My company is investing heavily in Stoneheart's future. We've acquired several properties in this area, with plans for revitalization that will benefit the entire community."

"How nice for you," I say, keeping my tone pleasant.

If he catches my sarcasm, he doesn't show it. "As part of our development strategy, we're particularly interested in established businesses with potential for growth." He slides a folder across my desk. "We'd like to make you an offer."

I don't touch the folder. "I'm not selling."

"You haven't even looked at the offer."

"Don't need to."

His smile tightens. "Ms. Sullivan, I understand you only recently acquired this establishment. Our offer would represent a significant profit on your investment. Quite possibly the best return you'll ever see."

Curiosity gets the better of me. I flip open the folder, and my eyebrows shoot up despite my best efforts. The number is obscene. Nearly triple what I've agreed to pay Devil if I still want the bar at the end of the next six months.

"That's... generous," I admit.

"We value what you've built here," he says smoothly. "The improvements you've made in such a short time are impressive. We see potential in this location that goes beyond its current... limitations."

My skin crawls as I realize he's had people in the bar since I've made the upgrades, checking it all out.

"Limitations?"

"Well." He gestures vaguely around us. "The building is old. The neighborhood is changing. Our development plans would revitalize the entire parcel of land with a focus on bringing in higher-end clientele, more foot traffic, and better revenue opportunities."

I close the folder, sliding it back across the desk. "I appreciate the offer, Mr. Crane, but I'm not interested. Devil's isn't just a building or a business to me. It's part of this community."

His pleasant expression doesn't waver, but something shifts in his eyes. "Community is precisely what we're trying to build, Ms. Sullivan. A better, safer, more prosperous Stoneheart for everyone."

"Everyone who can afford it," I counter.

"Progress always comes with change," he says smoothly. "Some adapt, some don't. But I'd encourage you to think about your future here. The town council is currently reviewing zoning regulations for this district."

My blood chills. "Is that so?"

"Absolutely. In fact, there's a proposal that would restrict liquor licenses in mixed-use developments, which is what this block is slated to become. Businesses that are already established might be grandfathered in, of course... but the change could trigger a review."

And there it is. The threat, thinly veiled but unmistakable.

"Are you suggesting that if I don't sell to you now, I might find myself unable to operate later?"

He holds up his hands. "Not at all. I'm simply sharing information that might be relevant to your business decisions. We'd hate to see you invest more in a property that might face... regulatory challenges."

I stand, making it clear our meeting is over. "I'll keep that in mind, Mr. Crane. But for now, Devil's isn't for sale."

"Of course." He stands as well, straightening his jacket. "The offer remains open. Here's my card, should you reconsider."

I take it just to get him moving. He's already overstayed his welcome.

"One more thing," he says, pausing at the office door. "I understand you've been hosting some... meetings here. With the local motorcycle club."

My face gives nothing away. "Devil's has always been open to the community."

"Of course." His smile is thin. "Just be careful about the company you keep, Ms. Sullivan. Some associations can complicate things unnecessarily."

"I'll choose my own associations, thanks," I say, my voice cooling several degrees. "Now, if there's nothing else?"

We exit back to the main bar area just as the door swings open, admitting Lee, Axel, and Cash. Their timing couldn't be worse—or better, depending on how you look at it.

Crane stiffens almost imperceptibly. Lee's eyes narrow as they clock the suit, then find me, a question in them that I can't quite answer.

"Gentlemen," Crane says with a nod as he edges toward the door. "Ms. Sullivan, consider our offer. I'll be in touch."

The bell over the door jingles as he leaves, the sound oddly cheerful in the tense silence he leaves behind.

Lee is at the bar in three long strides, his eyes burning with questions. "Who the hell was that?"

"David Crane. Summit Development." I reach under the bar for the bourbon, pouring myself a shot before offering the bottle to the men. "He came to make me an offer on the bar."

Axel's eyebrows shoot up. "Summit's moving on Devil's now?"

"Apparently." I knock back the shot, welcoming the burn. "Offered me three times what Devil asked for."

"And?" Lee's voice is tight.

I give him a flat look. "And I told him no."

The tension in Lee's shoulders eases slightly, but his scowl remains fixed. "What else did he want?"

"He mentioned the town council is reviewing zoning for this district. Something about restricting liquor licenses in mixed-use developments. Implied that if I didn't sell now, I might find myself unable to operate later."

"Fucking snakes," Cash mutters, accepting the glass I slide his way.

"He also mentioned my 'associations' with the club," I add. "Suggested I be careful about the company I keep."

Lee's hands clench into fists on the bar top. "They're watching us. And now you're on their radar."

"Because of the meetings you've been having here?" I ask.

"Maybe," Axel puts in. "But it's likely they had eyes on the place the moment Devil became interested in selling. This is fast, though. Even for them."

"I don't like it," Lee says, his voice dropping to a near-growl. "I don't like them sniffing around you."

His tone makes my hackles rise. "I can handle myself, Lee."

"Against Summit? Against the cartel?" He shakes his head. "This was a mistake. We should never have involved you. I'd like to drag Devil back here and—"

"Excuse me?" I plant my hands on the bar, leaning forward. "You didn't 'involve' me in anything. I chose to be a part of this town, and I'm choosing to be a part of this. My bar, my town, my choice."

"Your choice is going to get you hurt," he snaps. "These people don't play nice, Kya. They're ruthless. And now they've got their sights on you."

"So what's your solution? I should just roll over? Sell them the bar and skip town with my tail between my legs?" I glare at him. "That's not happening."

Lee runs a hand through his hair, frustration radiating from him. "Damn it, Kya. I'm trying to protect you."

"I don't need your protection." The words come out sharper than I intend. "I've been taking care of myself since I was old enough to reach the stove. I don't need you charging in like some leather-clad knight now."

Axel and Cash exchange a glance, clearly sensing they've wandered into personal territory.

"We should go," Axel murmurs to Cash, who nods quickly.

"Yeah." Cash slides off his stool, giving Lee a pointed look. "You coming, brother?"

Lee doesn't even look their way. "I'll catch up."

The two men make a hasty exit, the other customers doing the same. I call out a goodbye while locked in a staring contest with Lee and me.

"You're being stubborn," he says when the door closes behind on the final patron.

"And you're being condescending." I slam the bottle down harder than necessary. "Acting like I'm some helpless damsel who can't make her own decisions."

"I'm being realistic." His voice rises. "Summit isn't going to back off just because you told their suit to take a hike. They'll find other ways to pressure you. Dangerous ways."

"Let them try," I snap back, refilling my glass with shaking hands. "I'm not selling, and I'm not running. I'm done running from this town and the people in it."

"This isn't about your pride, Kya!" He slams his palm on the bar top, making the glasses shake. "These people can hurt you. And now they've got their sights on you because we brought you into this!"

"I brought myself into this!" I shout back, temper fully ignited now. "I don't need your permission, and I sure as hell don't need your guilt!"

Lee runs both hands through his hair, his eyes wild. "Damn it, Kya, why can't you just listen for once in your life?"

"Because that's how I survived!" The words explode out of me. "That's how I made it through growing up in this godforsaken town with a mother who couldn't take care of herself, let alone me."

His jaw clenches. "And how's that working out for you? Standing alone against the world?"

The question hits too close to home, striking a nerve I didn't realize was exposed. "Fuck you, Lee."

"Yeah, that's right. Shut me out. Push me away." He stands

abruptly, the stool scraping harshly against the floor. "God forbid anyone actually cares what happens to you."

"If you cared you'd respect my decisions instead of trying to make them for me."

"If you weren't so goddamn stubborn, you'd see I'm trying to keep you alive!"

"I never asked you to!"

The words hang in the air between us, sharp and dangerous. Lee stares at me, his chest heaving, eyes blazing. For a moment, I think he might say something else—something he can't take back—but then his expression shutters.

"Fine," he says, his voice suddenly cold and distant. "You want to handle this alone? Have at it. I won't waste my time trying to help someone who doesn't want it."

He turns and stalks toward the door, each step rigid with barely contained fury.

"Lee—" I start, already regretting how far this has escalated, but he cuts me off with a sharp gesture.

"Save it." His hand is on the door. "You've made your position clear. I won't bother you again."

The door slams behind him with enough force to rattle the windows. I stand frozen, adrenaline still coursing through my system, hands gripping the edge of the bar so tightly my knuckles turn white.

The silence that follows is deafening.

"Shit," I mutter, the anger draining out of me, leaving only a hollow ache in its place.

I shouldn't have pushed him like that. I know he was just worried. But something about Lee Armstrong has always made me defensive, made me want to prove I'm strong enough on my own.

Even when I'm not sure I am.

I clean the glasses with more force than necessary, trying to ignore the way my throat tightens and my eyes burn. I don't have time for this—for him, for these complicated feelings, for the tangle of emotions he stirs up.

My phone sits silent on the bar. No text this time.

And that hurts more than it should.

"Damn it," I whisper, turning away from the empty bar and the echo of words I can't take back. "Fucking men."

I have a business to run, bills to pay, and Summit Development to deal with. I don't have time for complicated feelings about Lee Armstrong.

7

LEE

The night air bites through my leather as I ride, the wind doing nothing to cool the anger still simmering under my skin. Hours after storming out of Devil's, my knuckles still ache from gripping the handlebars too tight, my jaw sore from clenching.

Stubborn. Infuriating. Impossible woman.

I'd spent the afternoon at the clubhouse, going over security plans with Stone and Axel, trying to focus on club business instead of replaying that argument in my head. But Kya's words kept echoing, sharp and defensive.

I don't need your protection.

Yes, she fucking does. The whole damn town needs the MC's protection right now. And maybe she doesn't want it, but that's just too bad. I'm not willing to see her hurt again.

The roads are quiet at this hour, most of Stoneheart already tucked in for the night. I take the long way home, letting the engine's rumble work through some of my frustration. The cold helps clear my head, and with each mile, my anger cools into something closer to regret.

I shouldn't have lost my temper. Shouldn't have pushed so hard.

But damn it, doesn't she understand what she's up against? Summit isn't some small-time operation she can face down with that sharp tongue and stubborn pride. They're dangerous—connected—and they don't take kindly to people standing in their way.

People like Kya.

I slow as I approach the familiar intersection, automatically glancing toward Devil's. The place should be dark—it's well past closing—but light spills from the windows, warm against the night's chill. Her car sits alone in the lot, the dented Subaru yet another relic she'd bought off Devil.

Before I can think better of it, I'm pulling in, killing the engine in front of the bar.

Just checking, I tell myself. Making sure everything's locked up tight. That's all.

The front door is locked when I try it, but I can hear music drifting faintly from inside, something old and bluesy that I can't quite place. I move around to the back entrance and find it unlocked, a sliver of light visible beneath.

Not smart, Kya. Not with Summit circling.

I push the door open carefully, alert for any sign of trouble. The music grows louder—Etta James, I realize—along with the distinctive smell of fresh paint.

I follow the scent down the back hallway, where I find her.

Kya stands on a stepladder, painting the upper portion of the wall a deep forest green. She's traded her usual jeans and top for paint-splattered overalls rolled up at the cuffs, her hair piled on top of her head in a messy bun. There's a smudge of paint on her cheek, and her bare feet peek out from beneath the frayed denim.

She looks younger like this, softer somehow. Less the defiant bar owner and more the girl I remember—the one who used to sit cross-legged on our porch swing with Emma, sharing secrets and laughter.

Something tightens in my chest at the sight.

I must make some noise because she turns, startled, nearly dropping her brush.

"Jesus!" She presses a hand to her chest. "You scared the hell out of me."

"Door was unlocked," I say by way of explanation. "Not exactly smart with Summit sniffing around."

Her expression closes off, walls going up so fast I can almost hear them slam into place. "I'm fine."

"Painting at midnight is your definition of 'fine'?"

"It's therapeutic." She turns back to her work, pointedly ignoring me. "What do you want, Lee?"

Good question. What am I doing here? Checking on her? Picking another fight?

Apologizing?

"Your car was the only one in the lot," I say, which isn't really an answer. "Wanted to make sure everything was okay."

"Everything's perfect." Her tone suggests the opposite.

I watch her paint for a moment, her movements precise despite the tension I can see in her shoulders. "You're doing the whole hallway yourself?"

"That was the plan." She doesn't look at me. "Unless the painting police are here to stop me."

I bite back a retort, remembering how well that approach worked earlier. Instead, I shrug out of my cut, folding it carefully and setting it on a nearby chair where it won't get splattered. "You got another brush?"

That gets her attention. She glances over her shoulder, surprise evident in her expression. "You're offering to help?"

"Unless you'd rather I leave."

She studies me for a long moment, like she's trying to decide if this is some kind of trick. "There's an extra brush in the paint tray. Grab the smaller ladder if you want the top half."

I do as instructed, setting up the ladder a few feet down from hers. We work in silence for a while, the only sounds are the soft music and the rhythmic swish of brushes against the wall. The quiet isn't exactly comfortable, but it's not hostile either. Just... cautious.

"I'm sorry," I say finally, focusing on a stubborn corner. "For earlier."

She doesn't respond right away, and I don't push. Just keep painting, giving her the space to reply or not.

"Me too," she says eventually, so quietly I almost miss it. "I shouldn't have gone off on you like that."

"You had every right to be pissed," I concede. "I was being overbearing."

"You were being protective," she corrects, dipping her brush in the paint. "I'm just not used to that."

The simple admission lands like a weight on my chest. Of course she's not used to it. Her mother was barely functional most days, and as far as I know, Patty Sullivan never had a relationship that wasn't either abusive or negligent. Who would have protected Kya growing up?

"Why'd you really come back?" I ask. "To Stoneheart, I mean. Besides dealing with your mom's estate."

She's quiet for so long I think she might not answer. Then she sighs, setting down her brush.

"I guess I was looking for something." She doesn't meet my eyes, gaze fixed on some distant point. "Connection, maybe. Belonging. I've moved around so much with my work, so I've never really found that. As messed up as this town was for me growing up, it's still the only place that ever felt like home."

The admission feels raw, vulnerable in a way Kya rarely allows herself to be.

"Why'd you buy the bar?"

She hesitates. "Honestly? I don't know."

I roll another layer onto the wall. "Seems like you'd be running the other way from here, what with all the bad memories."

She shrugs. "Not all of them are bad. Some are worth

keeping." Finally, she glances my way. "What about you? Why'd you stay? Join the club?"

It's my turn to consider the question. "Same reason, I guess. Belonging. Purpose." I dip my brush, focusing on the task. "After the army, I was... adrift. Couldn't figure out where I fit anymore. The club gave me that back."

"Does Emma ever visit?" she asks, changing the subject slightly.

"Christmas. Sometimes Thanksgiving." I shake my head, remembering my sister's last whirlwind visit. "She's always in a rush to get back to the city, though. This place is too small for her now."

"But not for you."

"Never was." I glance over at her. "Some of us are built for small towns. For community. For roots."

Something flickers across her face—recognition, maybe. Understanding. "Yeah. I tried the city thing. Had the fancy apartment, the IKEA furniture, the whole nine yards. But it never felt..."

"Real," I finish for her.

"Exactly." Her smile is small but genuine, the first one I've seen all night. "Nothing felt permanent. Just... temporary."

We fall back into silence, but it's lighter now, the tension easing with each stroke of our brushes. I find myself watching her when she's not looking, noticing the way she bites her lip in concentration, the curve of her neck as she reaches up, the stray wisps of hair curling against her skin.

Dangerous territory, Armstrong.

I clear my throat. "So what's the plan for this place? Besides turning it green?"

She glances around the hallway. "Fresh paint, some new fixtures, maybe update the bathrooms eventually. Nothing too fancy, I want to keep the soul of it intact. Just... freshen it up a bit."

"Suits it. How did you know the color to choose?" I ask, nodding toward the brush in her hand. Her painting style is all instinct—no tape, no measuring, just bold strokes and confidence. It's kind of hot.

"Gut instinct, mostly. I don't really overthink it. Just stand in the room until it tells me what it wants."

I raise an eyebrow. "The room talks to you?"

She grins at me. "In its own way. Every space has a mood, you know? Energy. History. My job is to coax that out and give it something to work with."

"Your job?" I echo. "This isn't just a hobby?"

"Nope," she says, stepping down from the ladder and stretching her back, revealing a stripe of skin between the hem of her tank and the dip in the side of the waistband of her overalls. "I flip houses."

That pulls me up short. "Seriously?"

"Seriously. Started a few years back in Portland. Saved every penny I had, worked three jobs at once—barista in the morning, waitress at night, part-time admin in between. Took me years to get a deposit together."

I let out a low whistle. "That's... damn impressive."

She shrugs, like it's no big deal, but I can tell she's proud. She should be. "It was hard. But once I bought my first place and flipped it, I got hooked. There's something about taking this broken thing that others have discarded and turning it into a beautiful home again."

"Is that why you bought Devil's?"

She tilts her head, considering. "Maybe. I think I saw something worth saving. Something that still had good bones. Plus... it was my mom's favorite place. For better or worse."

She pauses, a strange look crossing her face. "Actually, I think this is my way of feeling close to her," she says slowly, more to herself than to me. "When she was alive, I couldn't fix her. But working here, it feels good to be in the place she loved, even if that love was a toxic one." She shakes her head. "That's silly, right? That I should invest in the place an alcoholic loved best?"

Her words hit me right in the chest.

"I think you should do whatever you need to grieve and move forward. If that's burning this place to the ground or adding some paint to a wall, then do it."

She nods, tears shimmering on her lashes. "I loved her. But I hated what she became. What she did to me, to herself. And now she's gone and it's... confusing. It's grief, but it's also relief. And that feels like betrayal, even if I know it isn't."

I don't say anything. Just walk over and pull her gently into my arms. She comes willingly, folding into me like she's been waiting to be held together.

"It's not betrayal," I say against her hair. "It's the truth. And anyone who's ever loved an addict knows exactly what you mean. You can mourn the mother you had and the mother you needed. Both are real. Both deserve space."

She clings tighter for a beat before stepping back and wiping her eyes with the heel of her hand. "Sorry. That got heavy."

I pick up my brush, swiping it as I try to lighten the mood. "You want to know what I do?"

Her eyes flick toward me. "You mean you're not paid to brood in corners and be intimidating to shady businessmen?"

"Nope. Try again."

She taps a finger against her chin as if deep in thought. "Clown."

"I do look great in a red nose. But no."

"Lion tamer?"

"Feels like that sometimes with the prospects. Try again."

She snaps her fingers. "Male gigolo."

That startles a laugh out of me. Pulling my shirt up with one hand, I reveal my torso, watching as her gaze drops to my six pack. "Baby, no one can afford this deliciousness."

She swallows, and I'm gratified to see a flush touch her cheeks. I drop the shirt, grinning when her gaze finally meets mine.

She swallows once before shrugging. "Okay, I give up. Tell me."

"Security. I freelance—bodyguard work, property surveillance, sometimes transporting high-risk cargo."

"That sounds intense."

"It can be," I admit. "But it pays well, I get to travel to interesting places, and it gives me the freedom I need to serve the club."

"Freedom?" she echoes, her brow lifting.

"I don't like being tied down. Not by a schedule, not by a boss, not by someone breathing down my neck about clocking in at nine sharp. I like doing the job, doing it well, and then riding away when it's done."

She nods slowly. "Sounds lonely."

I meet her gaze. "Sometimes. But it also means I don't let anyone down."

That hangs there for a moment, heavier than I meant it. But she doesn't flinch. Doesn't look away.

She studies me a long beat, then drops a bomb. "You've never let me down."

My chest clenches as we stare at each other, the moment holding its breath.

Then she clears her throat and says, "Okay, enough therapy. Help me finish this wall before I turn into an emotional pancake."

"Deal," I say, grateful and reluctant all at once. "Should we order pizza or can we raid the kitchen?"

"I suspect neither is an option at this time of night."

"Damn." I hip bump her. "Guess you'll have to make it up to me later."

She glances over and her smile widens. "You've got paint on your face," she says, gesturing toward my cheek.

I swipe at it. "Better?"

"Worse." She laughs, the sound soft and genuine. "Now you look like you've got some kind of weird green beard growing."

"Speaking of faces with paint on them..." I flick my brush toward her, leaving a small green spatter across her cheek.

Her mouth drops open in exaggerated outrage. "You did not just do that."

"Did what?" I ask innocently, doing it again.

Her eyes narrow, and I see the exact moment she decides retaliation is necessary. She dips her brush, a dangerous gleam in her eye.

"Don't you dare," I warn, taking a step back.

"Oh, I dare." She flicks her brush, sending a spray of paint across my T-shirt.

And just like that, it's war.

I lunge for the paint tray, and she squeals, darting away as I load up my brush. We chase each other around the narrow hallway, laughing and dodging paint splatters like kids. Her earlier tension is gone, replaced by a playfulness I haven't seen since we were teenagers.

"You're going to regret this!" she warns, brandishing her brush like a weapon.

"I already do," I laugh, glancing down at my now-speckled jeans.

She makes a break for the main bar, and I catch her around the waist, spinning her around as she shrieks with laughter.

Her back hits the wall as I pin her in place, our faces inches apart. "Surrender?"

"Never," she declares, but her voice has lost its edge, going soft and breathy.

Time seems to slow. I'm suddenly acutely aware of every point of contact between us, my hands on her waist, her palms against my chest, the heat of her body through the thin fabric of her overalls. Her eyes, wide and golden in the dim light, drop to my mouth.

And something in me snaps.

Every moment since she walked back into Devil's—every heated glance, every challenging word, every time I caught myself watching the sway of her hips or the curve of her smile—crashes through me like a wrecking ball. The control I've been clinging to shatters, and I'm moving before I can think better of it.

My mouth finds hers in a kiss that's nothing like the careful, measured way I'd imagined doing this. It's raw, primal. A claiming. My fingers tangle in her hair, tilting her head back as I devour her, months of pent-up want breaking free at once. Her surprised gasp melts into a moan that vibrates through me, setting fire to my blood.

I press her harder against the wall, one hand sliding down to grip her hip, keeping her pinned against me. Her body is soft, yielding yet demanding as she arches into me, her hands fisting in my shirt like she's afraid I'll stop if she lets go.

God, she tastes amazing. Like whiskey and desire and everything I've been denying myself since she came back to town. I can't get enough. I deepen the kiss, my tongue tangling with hers in a battle for control neither of us seems interested in winning.

It's only when she makes a small, breathless sound that reality crashes back in. I tear my mouth from hers, breathing hard, horrified at how completely I just lost myself.

"Fuck," I mutter, taking half a step back. "Kya, I'm sorry. I didn't mean to—"

I run a hand through my hair, trying to gather my scattered thoughts. "That was... I shouldn't have..."

She stares at me, her lips swollen from my kiss, her eyes wide and dark with desire. I've never seen anything more beautiful, or more terrifying in what it makes me feel.

"Tell me to stop," I manage, giving her an out, giving us both a chance to pretend this never happened. "If you want me to stop, just say the word."

Instead, she curls her fingers into my shirt and pulls me closer.

"Shut up," she murmurs against my lips. "For once in your life, just shut up and kiss me, Lee."

I do. God help me, I do.

This time it's not a moment of lost control or a mistake. It's a choice—deliberate, intentional. Her hands slide into my hair, holding me to her as the kiss deepens, grows hungrier. I press her against the wall, lifting her, and her legs wrap around my waist, bringing us impossibly closer.

The paint on our hands and clothes is probably smearing everywhere, but I couldn't care less. All that matters is the heat of her mouth, the softness of her skin beneath my palms, the small sounds she makes when I trail kisses down her throat.

Her heat presses against me, separated only by two too-thin layers of clothing and a whole lot of bad decisions. I rock into her once—just to feel her. Her breath catches, her nails dig into my shoulders, and that's it. I lose the last shred of restraint.

I grind into her slowly, deliberately, pinning her harder to the wall with each roll of my hips. Every time I move, she gasps like it's a surprise, like she didn't think this would feel this good. This *right*.

I feel the exact moment her control snaps. She arches into me, moaning my name like a broken prayer. I grip her thighs tighter, help her ride the tension, every breath from her lips pulling me deeper.

Kya grinds against me, desperate and deliciously demanding, her breasts pressing into my chest with each roll of her hips. The sounds she makes—needy, breathless, raw—drive me half mad. I dip my head, dragging my mouth across her collarbone, tasting sweat, paint, and Kya.

She gasps again, her body tightening in my arms. She's close. I can feel it in the way her nails dig in, the frantic arch of her hips, the whispered fragments of my name spilling from her lips.

"That's it," I murmur, voice rough with hunger. "Let go for me, Kya. I've got you."

She breaks against me, the climax tearing through her in waves I feel as much as see. Her whole body shakes, her breath hitching as she buries her face in my neck.

I hold her through it, every muscle in my body screaming to take this further, to let go and get lost in her the way I've wanted for years. But I don't. I can't.

Not like this. Not when she deserves more than a wall and a fuck-ton of regret in the morning.

Slowly, gently, I ease her down, her legs shaky as they touch the floor. She leans into me, still trembling, and I press my lips to her forehead, forcing my own ragged breathing to slow.

"Good girl," I whisper, kissing her. "Hold on to me."

She doesn't pull away. Doesn't argue. Just rests her head against my chest and nods.

I don't move. Can't. Because letting go of her now might actually kill me.

Then, softly, barely above a whisper, she says, "If you ever tell anyone I came in my overalls while dry humping you, I will murder you in your sleep."

A surprised laugh punches out of me, sharp and unexpected. I lean back just enough to look at her, brushing a thumb under her chin until her eyes meet mine.

"Cross my heart," I promise. "It'll be our filthy little secret."

Her smile is slow, lazy, satisfied. She leans up, presses a kiss to my jaw, and whispers, "Next time? Lose the paintbrush first. And maybe your pants."

I groan, resting my forehead against hers. "You're gonna be the death of me."

"Worth it," she mutters.

And just like that, I know I'm already gone.

8

KYA

I wake up with paint in my hair, sore thighs, and the deeply uncomfortable knowledge that I made actual sex noises while dry humping a man fully clothed against a freshly painted wall.

Good job, Sullivan. Really keeping it classy.

I groan and flop back on the couch, covering my face with my forearm. My overalls—now crumpled and stiff with a combination of sweat, paint, and poor decision-making—are balled up in the laundry basket. Lee's hoodie—the one he wrapped around me before we left last night—still smells like him. I bury my face in it, inhaling deeply as if it's some kind of sinful security blanket. Which is deranged, frankly. Not to mention I shouldn't be this moony over a man that made me come so hard I nearly blacked out and then had the audacity to follow me home on his bike but refuse to come in. He kissed me at the door sweetly, though for a long fucking time, then gently told me to get some sleep.

The bastard.

To say I'm messy and emotionally constipated and apparently real into motorcycle club enforcers with tortured pasts is an understatement. Apparently, I'm gone for Lee Fucking Armstrong.

Damn it.

By the time I get to Devil's—coffee in hand, hair vaguely tamed—Mercy's already there, sorting liquor deliveries like the efficient menace she is.

She doesn't even look up when she says, "You're late."

"I'm ten minutes early."

"For you, that's late." She glances over and then straightens. "Whoa. Girl. Spill."

I blink. "What?"

She snorts. "You're got the face of someone who's either had sex, committed a murder, or both."

"I—what? No. I mean, definitely not a murder."

Mercy arches a perfectly sculpted brow. "Uh huh. Which means you've had sex."

"No, I haven't."

"Kya, you're wearing the same dreamy-dead-inside expression I get after three orgasms and a good pepperoni pizza."

I open my mouth. Close it. Sip my coffee. "You're deranged."

"And you're glowing." She sets down the bottle of bourbon with a thunk and crosses her arms. "Spill it, Sullivan."

There's no point fighting her. Apparently Mercy can smell sex like a bloodhound—a trait I wish I'd known before hiring her. I lean against the bar, trying to act casual. "I may have made out with someone last night."

She makes a buzzer sound. "Try again. Your skin is glowing, your pupils are dilated, and you've got that post-orgasm guilt that screams 'this man is a bad idea but I want to climb him like a jungle gym.' Spill it, sister."

"It was Lee."

Dead silence. Then—*slowly*—Mercy grins.

"Oh, babe."

I slap a hand over my face. "I know!"

"You finally climbed Mount Motorcycle."

"Mercy!"

She waggles her eyebrows and shimmies her shoulders. "I bet he left tread marks on your soul."

"I will unplug the jukebox and tell the regulars it's your fault."

She holds up her hands in surrender, but her grin doesn't dim. "So? Was it everything you imagined?"

"Better," I admit quietly. "But also... complicated."

"Go on."

I slump against the bar "Honestly, I've never been kissed like that."

"Like what?"

"Like I'm the last woman on Earth and he's dying to taste the air in my lungs."

She whistles, fanning herself. "Damn girl. And you? How'd you kiss him?"

I think back to our kiss, flushing. "About the same."

We stand in silence for a beat.

Finally, she speaks. "This is romantic as hell. Messy, but romantic."

"Is it? Cause at the moment it just feels confusing and a little overwhelming."

More than a little, if I'm honest.

"So," she says, straightening the coasters lying on the bar. "Are you going to talk to him?"

"I don't know."

"Kya."

"I don't want to make it weird."

Mercy gives me a long look. "Make what weird, exactly?"

"I don't know! I just… everything!" I wave my hands around to encompass the bar. "I'm only meant to be here for six months, and this is my focus, and I feel like falling for a badass biker is a terrible idea."

"Sure. Or it could be the best thing you ever do." She slaps a hand on the bar and pushes off. "Choice is yours."

She's right. Of course she is. Last night wasn't just some sex-adjacent nonsense. Or at least it wasn't for me.

I glance toward the back hallway—the one with paint still drying on the walls—and sigh.

"You want some unsolicited advice?" Mercy asks, her tone gentler now.

"Do I have a choice?"

"Nope." She leans against the bar, studying me. "I was married for eight years to a man who was everything I thought I wanted on paper. Stable job, nice house, looked good at dinner parties. Seemed safe."

I look up, surprised. Mercy's never mentioned being married.

"What happened?"

"It was suffocating," she says simply. "He had opinions about everything—what I wore, who I talked to, how I spent my time, where I could work. Made me feel like I was shrinking smaller and smaller until I barely recognized myself. Then I met Jake. He was a traveling musician with tattoos and a motorcycle, and absolutely no business sense whatsoever."

"Did you leave your husband for him?"

"Nope. I left my husband for me." She picks up a glass, polishing it absently. "Jake made me remember what it felt like to laugh, to feel free, to be myself without someone constantly watching and judging. I didn't realize how controlled my life had become until I met someone who didn't try to manage every breath I took."

"What happened with Jake?"

Her smile is bittersweet. "Nothing. I'm not a cheater. He was simply the catalyst to me recognizing that I needed to change my life. We all deserve happy."

My throat tightens. "Mercy, I'm sorry."

"Don't be. I'm not." She sets down the glass and looks at me directly. "Point is, some people are worth the risk. And from what I saw the other night—the way that man looked at you like you hung the moon—Lee might be one of them."

I want to argue and point out all the reasons this is complicated, but the words stick in my throat.

"He's not going anywhere, Kya," she continues. "This is his home. The question is whether you're brave enough to see where this goes, or if you're going to run back to the safety of Portland."

The accusation stings because it hits too close to home. "I'm not running."

"Aren't you?" She raises an eyebrow. "You've been back how long? A few weeks? In that time you've bought a bar, signed a lease, but you're still talking about this being temporary. Sounds like denial to me."

Before I can respond, she pushes off the bar. "I'm going to finish the inventory. Think about what I said."

She disappears into the back, leaving me alone with my thoughts and a growing knot in my stomach.

The front door chimes, and I look up to see three women enter. One with dark brown-red hair that catches the light and an edge to her that screams "don't mess with me." The other has long dark hair pulled back in a messy braid and warm eyes that match her smile. Behind them struts a gorgeous redhead in a top so low-cut I'm amazed nothing's fallen out.

"You must be Kya," the "don't mess with me" woman says, approaching the bar with a surprisingly warm smile. "I'm Andi, Hawk's wife. This is Poppy—she's engaged to Axel."

The redhead slides onto a barstool with feline grace. "And I'm Ginger. Tank's old lady, resident troublemaker, and the one who's been dying to meet the girl who's got Lee Armstrong twisted in knots."

I recognize their names immediately. Hawk's the Sergeant at Arms, Axel's the Road Captain, and Tank's the Vice President. These are the women who came before me in this world of leather and loyalty.

"Ladies," I say, straightening. "What can I get you?"

"Just Diet Cokes," Poppy says, settling onto a barstool. Her smile is just as warm as Andi's, and I like them both immediately. "But we're not here to drink. We're here to meet you."

"Speak for yourself," Ginger interrupts. "I'll take a shot of tequila. It's five o'clock somewhere, and mommy needs her medicine."

Andi rolls her eyes. "It's two in the afternoon."

"Your point?" Ginger winks at me. "Pour yourself one too, honey. We need to discuss how you've got that boy so wrapped around your finger he's practically gift-wrapped."

I pour their drinks, hyper-aware that I'm being evaluated. "Oh?"

"Don't worry, everything is so far, so good," Andi says, accepting her glass. "We're not here to give you the third degree. We just wanted to invite you to a party at the clubhouse tonight. Nothing fancy, just family getting together."

Ginger knocks back her shot and leans forward, giving me an eyeful of cleavage. "Translation, the boys will get drunk, we'll gossip, and someone will definitely end up naked in the pool. Last time it was our Prospect, Steel. Poor boy still hasn't recovered."

I'm intrigued but I still frown, confused. "Why?"

They exchange a look. "Why not? Parties are fun, Lee is hot, and we want to get to know you."

"Plus," Ginger adds, wiggling her eyebrows, "I have a bet with Tank about whether you two will sneak off to neck before or after dinner. I've got fifty on before."

"Ginger!" Poppy gasps, but she's fighting a laugh.

That pulls a reluctant smile from me.

Andi leans in a little. "Also, the food's going to be amazing. Come for the eye-candy, stay for the brisket."

"I don't know."

"Come," Ginger purrs. "There's nothing like watching grown men try to prove who's tougher after a few beers. Last party, Bones tried to bench press his bike."

Before I can respond, the door to the storeroom swings open and Mercy strides out, a clipboard in one hand.

"You should go," she says, pointing her pen at me. "All work and no play makes Kya a bad boss."

"I can't, the bar—"

"I'll cover your shift tonight."

"Mercy, no."

"You heard me." She glances up, eyes narrowing just slightly. "You've been working nonstop since you took this place on. Take the damn night off. Go flirt with your man, eat too much food, have fun for once."

"And if you're really lucky, you'll get to see Lee without his shirt." Ginger gives a little shimmy that has her hair and breasts shaking. "Trust me, it's worth the price of admission."

Andi grins. Poppy lifts her Diet Coke like a toast.

Seeing that I'm outnumbered, I give in.

"Okay, fine. I'll go." I lean against the bar, glancing between them. "But there's one problem."

"And that is?" Poppy asks.

"What am I going to wear?"

Ginger's eyes light up like Christmas morning. "Oh honey, now you're speaking my language. How do you feel about leather?"

9

KYA

I stand in front of my bedroom mirror, second-guessing my outfit choice. Dark jeans hug my curves, a black fitted top shows just enough cleavage to be interesting without being obvious, and my favorite leather jacket.

Feels like it's appropriate for a motorcycle club party... Maybe?

The drive to the clubhouse takes fifteen minutes, and with every mile, my nerves ratchet higher. What if I don't fit in? What if they're just being polite but don't actually want me there?

The front door opens before I can talk myself out of it, and Andi, Poppy, and Ginger appear together, clearly having been watching for me.

"There she is!" Poppy calls out, practically bouncing down the steps. "I was starting to think you'd chickened out."

"Almost did," I admit, getting out of my car.

Ginger wolf-whistles. "Damn girl, you clean up nice. Lee's gonna swallow his tongue."

Andi grins, taking in my outfit with an approving nod. "You look fantastic. Come on, let's get you inside before you lose your nerve completely."

They flank me as we head toward the door, Ginger linking her arm through mine. "Fair warning - Tank's already three beers in and challenging people to arm wrestle. Steel's playing referee and losing badly."

Sure enough, as we step inside, I spot Tank at a table, his massive frame dwarfing the prospect beside him—Steel, who's trying to maintain order while Tank flexes dramatically.

"STEEL!" Tank bellows. "Tell this punk I won fair and square!"

Steel looks like he'd rather be anywhere else. "You cheated. You can't tickle someone during arm wrestling."

"Show me where that's in the rules!" Tank grins wickedly.

My eyes automatically scan the crowded room looking for Lee.

Desperate much?

I find him by the bar, talking with Cash and Bones. When our eyes meet across the room, everything else fades away. The conversations, the music, the chaos—it all becomes background noise as he excuses himself and starts making his way toward me.

"Oh, you've got it bad," Andi murmurs beside me, following my gaze.

"Is it that obvious?"

"Honey, you're practically glowing," Poppy laughs. "And he looks like he's about to devour you whole."

"I'm adding oral to our bet. There's no way they're making it to dinner," Ginger stage-whispers to Tank as he joins us.

"You're on," Tank says, wrapping an arm around Ginger. "My boy's got more self-control than that."

"Better warm up that tongue. Your boy's been eye-fucking her since she walked in," Ginger retorts.

He flicks it out at her then laughs when she elbows him in the gut.

Lee reaches us, and without a word, he slides an arm around my waist, pulling me against his side. The possessive gesture sends heat shooting through me.

"Ladies," he says, though his eyes never leave mine. "Mind if I steal her for a minute?"

"We were attempting to get to know her," Poppy starts, but there's a smile in her voice. "But, sure. Go ahead. Steal our new friend."

"Looks like Ginger's winning the bet," Andi says with a grin.

Before I can protest, Lee's guiding me through the crowd, his hand warm and sure on my back. He leads me to a quiet corner near the back windows, away from the main party.

"Hi," he says softly, turning to face me fully.

"Hi yourself."

"You came."

"You doubted I would?"

"Maybe a little." His hands settle on my waist, thumbs brushing along my ribs. "You look fucking incredible, by the way."

The praise makes my chest tight. "Lee..."

He leans in, his mouth brushing my ear. "You take my breath away, you know that?"

My breath catches.

His hands slide up, thumbs stroking just beneath the edge of my top, teasing against skin. "I watched you walk through that door and forgot how to fucking think. You look like trouble, Kya."

I flush, thighs clenching involuntarily.

"You're nervous," he murmurs, voice low and wicked. "But you still showed up. Good girl."

My heart's hammering. I can't breathe. I can barely stand still under the weight of his gaze.

"Say the word," he says, brushing his lips along my jaw. "I'll take you upstairs right now, lay you out, and show you exactly what it means to be worshipped. Or..." His teeth nip gently at my neck, just once. "We can stay down here and pretend like I'm not thinking about you with my mouth on your thighs."

I sway toward him without meaning to. His hands hold me steady.

"Why are you like this?" I whisper, breathless.

"You make me like this," he murmurs.

"Ahem."

We both turn, to find Poppy standing behind us with a smug smile and a raised brow. Her eyes flick between us, assessing, amused.

"Sorry to interrupt the smolder-fest," she says, not sounding remotely sorry, "but there's a Fleetwood Mac remix playing. You, my darling, are coming to dance with us."

"And do shots!" Ginger adds cheerfully.

Lee's brows lift. "You mind? We're busy here."

"Shut up, you animal," Poppy laughs, grabbing my wrist. "You can go back to eye-fucking her later. Right now, she's mine."

Tank claps Lee on the shoulder. "Come on, brother. Let the women have their fun. Steel's about to demonstrate his interpretation of 'dancing.' You don't want to miss this."

"I don't dance," Steel protests.

"You do tonight," Ginger says, handing him a shot. "That's what prospects are for, entertainment!"

Lee chuckles as I glance back, torn between staying in his gravity and letting myself get pulled into something lighter. But Poppy's infectious grin makes the choice easy.

"I'll come back," I promise Lee.

"I'll hold you to it," he says, and there's something in his eyes that makes the promise feel heavier than the words.

The next hour is a blur of laughter, dancing, and clinking glasses. Poppy is a terrible influence and an even worse drinking buddy—in that she constantly refills my glass but never takes a shot of her own. I come to find out around shot three that she's close to twelve weeks pregnant. Maybe she isn't a crappy drinking buddy after all.

Andi joins us halfway through a song and suddenly we're all swaying together in a loose triangle, hips moving to the music, shouting lyrics like we're back in college.

Somewhere between the fourth and sixth tequila shot, I lose track of my worries.

The music pulses through the clubhouse, the lights low and warm, bodies moving everywhere. I'm sweaty, breathless, and tipsy enough that I keep laughing at things that aren't that funny.

"This is the best worst idea ever," I shout to Poppy over the music.

"I know!" she beams. "Wait till Bones gets drunk. That bitch can do the worm."

I snort and nearly spill my drink. That's when I feel it—a hand, large and steady, pressing against the small of my back.

I turn and there he is.

Lee.

"Hey," he says, voice low enough that I have to lean in to hear it.

"Hey yourself."

"You good?"

I nod. Maybe too quickly as the world tips a fraction. "I'm... very hydrated."

His mouth twitches, and he slides his arm around my waist. "You ready to go home?"

I nod again. This time slower. "Yeah."

He glances at Poppy and Andi. "I'm stealing her."

"She's all yours," Poppy says, still dancing. "Just bring her back next week."

Lee keeps a careful hand on my back as we weave through the crowd. By the time we make it to my car, the night air is cool on my flushed skin.

"We're not riding?" I ask, disappointed.

"Babe, you can barely stand."

"You'll catch me."

He smirks. "Always. But I'm not risking you getting gravel rash."

A low rumble of an engine sounds behind us, and I glance back to see one of the prospects pulling up in a beat-up truck.

"I asked him to follow," Lee says, nodding toward the prospect. "That way we can drop your car home."

Lee opens the passenger door of my car and helps me in.

When he slides into the driver's seat, the car is quiet except for the low hum of the engine and the pounding of my heart.

"Thanks," I murmur, not entirely sure what I'm thanking him for.

He reaches over and brushes a strand of hair behind my ear, his fingers grazing my cheek. "Anytime, baby."

The drive back to my house is slow, taking far longer than the fifteen minutes it should. Lee's hand rests on my knee, sliding slowly up my thigh.

By the time we pull into my driveway, I'm aching.

Lee parks, gets out, and is already at my side, helping me out as if he's a gentleman—which feels dangerous coming from a man who's looked at me like a sinner all night.

We walk up the front steps together, his hand on the small of my back.

At the door, I fumble with the keys, nervous.

"Kya."

I pause, looking up at him.

He leans in, slow and sure, his hand cupping the side of my face. "You wreck me. You know that?"

My breath catches. "Lee—"

His mouth claims mine.

The kiss is deep and slow, deliberate. A promise. A question. His other hand slides to my waist, pulling me closer, and I melt into him, clinging to the front of his shirt like it's the only thing keeping me upright.

When we finally break apart, I'm breathless. Dizzy. Wanting.

"Come in," I whisper.

His forehead presses to mine. "I want to. So fucking badly."

"Then—"

He pulls back just enough to shake his head, gently brushing his thumb across my lips.

"Not like this," he says. "You've been drinking. You deserve better than something you might regret in the morning."

I swallow, heart thudding. "I wouldn't."

He smiles. "Still not happening. But soon, baby. Real soon."

He kisses me once more, quick and firm, then takes the keys and opens my door.

"Lock up after me," he says, voice low.

"Text me when you get home?"

He nods, already backing away. "Always."

I watch him walk down the steps, my heart in my throat. He waits until I'm inside before driving away.

I am in *so* much trouble.

10

KYA

I wake with a dry mouth and a racing heart, blinking against the sunlight that filters through my bedroom curtains. The tequila lingers in my bloodstream like a bad decision—fuzzy, warm, and laced with fragments of last night.

Dancing. Laughter. Lee.

His hands on me. His mouth on mine. The promise in his voice. *Soon, baby. Real soon.*

I groan and bury my face in the pillow.

The temptation to text him is immediate and overwhelming. I grab my phone from the nightstand and stare at our last messages. My fingers hover over the keyboard.

KYA

Hey, about last night...

Delete.

KYA

I've been thinking about what happened

Delete.

KYA

Can we talk?

Too desperate. Delete.

KYA

Thanks for bringing me home last night. And thanks for helping with the painting and… other stuff.

God, that sounds like I'm twelve and can't openly talk about an orgasm. Which, technically, is true—not the twelve part, but the talking about orgasms with Lee part. Delete.

I set the phone down with a frustrated sigh and begin to get ready for work. Possible scenarios run through my head as I shower, eat breakfast and drive to the bar.

Normally when I'm surrounded by the quiet buzz of the fridge and the distant hum of the street I calm. Not today. Nothing seems to help. I rearrange the bottles behind the bar by height, then by color, then by how much alcohol they contain. I move to the tables, straightening chairs that are already perfectly aligned and checking saltshakers that don't need checking.

My phone buzzes, and I lunge for it like a lunatic.

UNKNOWN

Your car is due for its 12 month warranty check. Book in now to save 10% off your next service.

"Pathetic," I mutter, shoving the phone back in my pocket.

But I can't stop thinking about what Mercy said yesterday.

Am I running?

The plan was always to stay six months. Sell the bar. Handle Mom's estate. Figure out what to do with the money.

Except... when was the last time I felt as alive as I did last night, pressed against the door with Lee's hands on me and his mouth claiming mine?

When was the last time someone looked at me like I was *it* —not a mess, not a project, not a one-night fix—but *it*?

Never. That's when.

My phone feels like it weighs a thousand pounds in my pocket. I pull it out again, staring at Lee's name.

This time, I just type.

KYA

Are you free tonight?

Before I can second-guess myself, I hit send.

The response comes back almost immediately.

LEE

For you? Always.

My heart does some kind of complicated flip—part relief, part terror, part excitement I'm not ready to examine too closely.

KYA

Good. We need to talk.

LEE

Devil's?

KYA

My place. If that's okay?

LEE

I'll be there.

I stare at the phone for a long moment, then shove it back in my pocket.

Yeah, we're going to talk. But first, I'm going to have to figure out what the hell I want to say.

11

KYA

I vacuum the same patch of carpet for the third time before accepting that it's already spotless. The cottage is cleaned to within an inch of its life—baseboards scrubbed, windows gleaming, even the inside of the microwave sparkles. The scent of lemon cleaner hangs in the air, tickling my nose.

Everything is spotless except my bedroom. My bed looks like a clothing store exploded. Five different outfits lie crumpled across the comforter—too casual, too dressy, too obvious, too frumpy, too much cleavage. I'm currently wearing dark leggings and a soft gray sweater that hits me mid-thigh, but I've changed my mind about it at least twice in the last ten minutes.

This isn't a date, *technically*. Lee is just coming over to talk. To figure out what the hell happened last night and what it means going forward.

The rational part of my brain is screaming that this is a terrible idea. That getting involved with Lee Armstrong is asking for complications I don't need. It's telling me to stick to my plan—six months, sort out the bar, figure out my life, move on.

But the rest of me? The part that's been dormant for years until he kissed me against that paint-splattered wall? That part is practically vibrating with anticipation.

My phone buzzes on the kitchen counter.

LEE

Outside.

My heart does that annoying flip-flopping thing it's been doing all day. In a slight panic, I scoop up the discarded outfits and throw them into the closet, stuffing them out of sight. Then I take a breath, smooth down my sweater with sweaty palms, check my reflection in the mirror one last time, and walk to the front door.

When I open it, Lee is leaning against the doorframe, helmet tucked under one arm, dark hair slightly mussed from the ride. He's wearing his cut over a simple black long-sleeved T-shirt and worn jeans. He looks like trouble.

"Hey," he says, voice low and warm, eyes searching my face.

"Hey," I echo awkwardly, stepping aside to let him in.

He enters slowly, taking in the small space with its cozy living room and second-hand furniture, the kitchen table that's seen better days, the stack of house-flipping magazines on the coffee table. For a rental, it's nothing fancy. But then up until this point I've assumed I'm leaving.

"Nice place," he says, and I can tell he means it.

"Thanks. It's a rental, but it works." The word *temporary* hovers between us, unsaid. Everything in my life is temporary lately.

We stand there in the quiet hum of the cottage's heater, neither of us sure how to begin. The easy banter from last night feels a million miles away.

"Do you want a drink?" I finally ask, because my hands need something to do and my throat is suddenly dry.

"Sure."

I pour two glasses of the good whiskey from the bottle I've been saving for a special occasion. Though I'm not sure if this occasion qualifies as such. I hand him a glass, our fingers brushing in the exchange, and that simple contact sends heat shooting up my arm.

We don't toast. Just drink.

The whiskey burns, but it's a good burn.

"So," I start, perching on the edge of my couch.

"So," he echoes, settling beside me but leaving space between us. Not much space, but enough that I'm acutely aware of it.

Lee sets down his glass, turning to face me fully. The careful distance he's been maintaining disappears as he shifts closer.

"Last night..." he starts, then stops, running a hand through his hair. "Fuck. I've been thinking about it all day."

"Yeah?"

He looks at me—really looks at me—with an intensity that makes my breath catch. "Let me correct that. I've been thinking about *you* all day."

My heart and stomach do simultaneous flips.

"What's going on between us isn't just heat-of-the-moment stuff for me, Kya. I mean, it started like that, but it was also..." He pauses, searching for words. "I think maybe I never really saw you before."

"Lee—"

"No, let me say this." His voice is rough, honest. "I've been fighting this since the day I knew you were back in town. But I can't anymore. I don't want to."

Relief floods through me at his admission, but it's quickly followed by fear. "But it scares me," I whisper.

"Why?" His hand reaches out, fingers barely grazing mine on the couch between us.

I laugh, but there's no humor in it. "Where do I start? You're Emma's brother. You're a biker. I'm only supposed to be here for six months. We have history that's... complicated. And I have a track record of making spectacularly bad decisions when it comes to men."

He turns to face me fully. "What kind of bad decisions?"

Heat rises in my cheeks. "The kind where I fall for guys who are emotionally unavailable, or controlling, or just plain wrong for me. I'm so screwed up I ignore every red flag because I think I can fix them."

"You think I need fixing?"

"No," I say quickly. "That's not... God, this is coming out all wrong." I tap my fingers on my knee, frustrated. "I just mean that my judgment when it comes to relationships is questionable at best. And this—whatever this is—it feels big."

Not to mention I've had a crush on the guy since I was a tween. If this goes sideways, I'm not sure I'll recover.

Lee is quiet for a long moment, studying me. "What if we don't screw it up?"

"What if we do?"

"Then we deal with it." He reaches over, taking my hand in his. His fingers are warm, callused from work and riding. "Kya, I'm not some kid with commitment issues. I know what I want."

"And that is?"

His thumb traces over my knuckles. "You. I'm not saying we'll be together forever, it's too early for us to know that. But I want a relationship with you. I wanna see where this might lead."

"I want that too," I admit. "But I'm terrified."

"Of what?"

"Of staying. Of leaving. Of caring too much and getting hurt." I look down at our joined hands. "Of being happy and having it ripped away."

Understanding flickers in his eyes. "Like with your mom."

I nod, throat tight. "She was the only family I had. And even though our relationship was complicated and painful, losing her... it reminded me how alone I am."

"I'm not going anywhere, Kya."

"You say that now—"

"I'm not going anywhere," he repeats, firmer this time. "This is my town. My family. My life."

I set my glass down, suddenly restless. "This feels too easy. I'm waiting for the other shoe to drop."

"What other shoe?"

I gesture between us. "This. You being here, saying everything I've ever wanted to hear. It feels too good to be real."

Lee reaches for my hands, his touch grounding me. "Can't real be good?"

"I don't know," I admit. "I've spent so long protecting myself, building walls. I don't know how to just... be happy."

"Maybe we figure it out together."

Something in his voice makes me look up, really look at him. There's vulnerability there I've never seen before.

"What are you most afraid of?" I ask.

He's quiet for a long moment, his thumbs tracing over my knuckles. "Becoming my father. Caring so much about someone that losing them breaks something in me that may never heal."

I wince. "Your mother?"

He shakes his head. "Emma. He loves us more than he ever loved her. Whatever was between them soured long before she and Emma went to New York."

I hesitate. "I'm afraid of turning into my mother. I'm terrified of needing someone—or something—so much that I lose myself completely."

"The alcohol?"

I nod. "I think being behind the bar gives me a sense of control. I definitely need a therapist."

We both smile at my half-assed joke.

"Come here." He pulls me gently into his side. My head finds his shoulder and his arm wraps around me, steady and warm. His fingers drift up to my hair, tangling lightly in the strands and combing them back in soft, absent strokes.

"I'm not going to lie, Kya. I've spent my whole adult life avoiding relationships," he says quietly. "I watched my dad fall apart. Watched him try to hold the family and club together while dealing with his own pain. And I swore I'd never put myself in that position. Never care about someone so much that losing them could destroy me."

"But you do care," I say softly. "About the club and your family."

He looks at me with an expression so raw it makes my chest ache. "Yeah. Turns out I'm pretty shit at keeping promises."

I smile. "That I can't believe."

His fingers tangle in my hair, gently gliding through the strands.

"If we do this, what do you see our life like?" I ask, curious.

He's quiet for a beat, then murmurs against my temple, "Morning coffee together talking about our days. Your feet in my lap while you scroll on your phone and pretend not to watch the game in the evenings."

I smile. He continues, voice low and rough now.

"Fights about whose turn it is to do dishes... and then making up on the kitchen counter."

I laugh softly, and he leans in, his nose brushing mine.

"Coming home to you covered in paint or sawdust or whatever mess you've decided to fix that day, and knowing you're mine. Waking up tangled around you, every damn morning. Falling asleep the same way every night."

His hands frame my face, thumbs brushing over my cheekbones. "I want a partner who'll listen to the hard shit, and stand with me. I want you to fall in love with the club, knowing you'll have a place with them as much as you do with me."

He leans in. "And yeah," he finishes, lips brushing my cheek, "hot sex. Lots of it. But that's the bonus, not the reason."

I'm not sure if it's the words or the way he says them, but a lump lodges in my throat. Some deep ache of hope I didn't realize I was still carrying.

"You really think we could have that?" I whisper.

"Yeah, baby."

"Even though we're both terrified?"

"Especially because we're both terrified." His mouth curves in a small smile. "Means it matters."

When he kisses me, it's soft at first. A question more than a demand. I answer by melting into him, my hands sliding up his chest to wrap around his neck.

The kiss deepens gradually, heat building like a slow burn. He tastes like whiskey and every secret I've ever wanted to tell. His hands slide down to my waist, pulling me closer, and I can feel the steady beat of his heart against my chest.

He shifts me until I'm sitting on his lap, my thighs on either side of his, my chest lined up to his.

His hands map the curve of my waist, the line of my spine, never rushing, never demanding more than I'm giving. When his fingers slip under the hem of my sweater to find bare skin, I shiver at the contact.

"You okay?" he murmurs against my lips.

"More than okay," I whisper back.

We stay like that for what feels like hours—kissing, touching, talking in whispered fragments between heated moments. He tells me about his first deployment, the way the desert made everything feel both infinite and claustrophobic. I tell him about my first house flip, how I cried when the buyers moved in because it felt like giving away a piece of myself.

We learn each other slowly. The scar on his shoulder from a motorcycle accident when he was nineteen. The way my breath catches when he kisses the spot just below my collarbone. How he laughs when I trace the tattoo on his forearm. How I melt when he says my name as I bite his earlobe.

"Tell me about Portland," he says after a while, his fingers tracing lazy patterns on my arm.

"What do you want to know?"

"Everything. Your life there. Your friends. What made you happy."

I think about it, surprised to realize how little there is to tell. "I had a nice apartment. A routine. I was good at my job."

"That's not what I asked."

I'm quiet, searching for something more substantial. "I had some friends from work. We'd go to happy hour sometimes. I dated a little, but nothing serious. I volunteered at a community garden on weekends."

"Sounds lonely."

The observation stings because it's true. "I didn't think it was at the time."

He brushes my hair back, tucking it behind my ear. "I told you what I want from this relationship. Now it's your turn."

I rest my forehead against his, breathing him in. "I want mornings with you," I say quietly. "But I want the kind where we argue about who used the last of the cereal and then end up making out in front of the fridge."

His eyes warm, that hint of a smirk tugging at the corner of his mouth.

"I want to come home to you, but I also want us to be the

kind of couple who knows when we each need space, but still finds a way to reach for each other."

I brush my thumb along his jaw. "I want to fall asleep with your hand on my hip and your bike outside the door. I want no-shirt Sundays so I can lick your chest."

He chuckles.

"I want to look up from the bar and see you there, waiting for me. I want…" I swallow, forcing myself to admit what's in my heart. "I want to know that I'm yours and you're mine."

Before he can interrupt, I rush on. "I want to come home to you grumbling about club politics while I hand you a beer. And yeah, I want the hot as fuck sex as well."

He leans his forehead against mine. "Sounds good to me."

He kisses me again. Slowly but deeply, this teeth nipping at my bottom lip.

The heat between us ramps up, but to my ever-loving frustration, he keeps us firmly at second base… and above the clothes.

Despite my best efforts, he slows us down.

"Why?" I ask, knowing I sound just the tiniest bit petulant.

He leans forward, nipping my earlobe as he answers, his breath hot against my skin. "I want to build the kind of anticipation that has you soaked and shaking, When I finally slide into you, Kya, you'll be begging me to make you come."

I shudder. "I could beg now."

Lee chuckles, relaxing back onto the couch. "Don't deny me this. I want to tease us both for a while."

We fall into comfortable silence, the only sounds the steady beat of his heart and the distant hum of traffic. After a while my eyelids grow heavy, the stress and emotion of the last few days finally catching up with me.

"I should probably go," Lee says, but he doesn't move.

"Probably," I agree, but I don't let go of him either.

"Let me stay," he says after a moment. "Just to sleep. I don't like the idea of you being alone."

I know I should say no, but the truth is, I don't want to be alone either.

"Okay."

We make our way to my bedroom, the domesticity of it both thrilling and terrifying. He borrows a toothbrush, I change into pajamas in the bathroom, and then we're lying in my bed in the dark. He's taken his shirt and jeans off, leaving him in just his briefs.

To say watching that was a religious experience is an understatement. The man could give a god a run for his money.

"This is crazy," I murmur into the darkness.

"Yeah," he agrees, pulling me closer. "But good crazy."

His hand finds mine under the covers, lacing our fingers together. It's a simple gesture, but it feels monumental.

"Sleep, Kya," he murmurs against my hair. His hand slips up to rest on my hip.

Closing my eyes, I smile.

12

LEE

I wake up to the soft, unfamiliar rhythm of someone else's breathing. For a second, I forget where I am—the bed beneath me isn't mine, the room smells like vanilla and something I can't place. Then I feel the weight against my chest, the warmth pressed along my side.

Kya.

Her hair is a mess of blonde waves across my shirt, one hand splayed over my ribs, the other still tangled with mine under the covers. Fuck, she feels good snuggled in beside me. I've had women in my bed before, but this is different.

She's different. Or maybe I am because she's mine.

The possessiveness that thought brings should scare me. Instead, it settles a restlessness I've carried for years. Her lashes flutter against my chest, and I watch her surface slowly from sleep. I tighten my arm around her waist, selfish enough to want to keep her here just a little longer.

"Morning, sunshine," I murmur against her hair.

She makes a sound that's part groan, part death rattle. "Do not sunshine me before coffee, Armstrong. I will end you."

I chuckle, the vibration making her grumble and burrow deeper into my chest. "Noted. You're not a morning person."

"I'm not a people person before ten a.m. and two cups of coffee," she mutters into my shirt. "Consider yourself warned."

"What if I'm very, very charming?" I ask, cupping her ass.

She lifts her head just enough to glare at me with one squinted eye. Her hair is sticking up in about seventeen different directions, there's a crease from the sheet pressed into her cheek, and she's never looked more beautiful.

"Charming is not going to save you from my morning wrath," she says, but she's fighting a smile.

"What about devastatingly handsome?"

"Strike two."

"Irresistibly sexy?"

She snorts. "You're pushing your luck, biker boy."

I lean down to kiss her, but she plants a hand on my chest and pushes me back with surprising strength.

"Absolutely not," she says firmly. "I have heinous morning breath. Like, could-kill-a-small-animal levels of bad."

"I don't care—"

"I care. For both our sakes." She covers her mouth with her hand, glaring at me over her fingers. "No kissing these lips until I've brushed my teeth. That's the rule."

I study her face, taking in the self-consciousness hiding behind the humor. Then I grin, slow and wicked.

"Fine," I say, sliding down in the bed.

Before she can ask what I'm up to, I push up her oversized sleep shirt and press my mouth to the soft skin just below her ribs. She gasps, her hand flying to my hair.

"Lee—"

"You said no mouth kissing," I murmur against her skin, trailing kisses across her stomach. "You didn't say anything about kissing other places."

Her laugh turns breathless as I work my way up, pressing soft kisses to the curve of her breast through her thin camisole. "That's... that's not what I meant and you know it."

"Sue me," I say, grinning up at her. "I'm a problem solver."

She's trying to look stern, but her fingers are already threading through my hair, holding me closer instead of pushing me away. "You're trouble."

"The best kind," I agree, pressing one more kiss to her collarbone before flopping back down beside her. "But I'll behave. For now."

She shakes her head, but she's smiling now, the self-consciousness replaced by something warmer. "You're insufferable."

"And you're beautiful," I say simply.

Pink floods her cheeks. "I look like I got hit by a truck."

"You look like you spent the night being thoroughly kissed

by someone who's crazy about you," I correct. "Which you did."

She buries her face in her hands. "God, we're disgustingly cute, aren't we?"

"Disgustingly," I agree, tugging her hands away from her face. "I'm thinking about making you pancakes. That's how far gone I am."

Her eyes light up. "You know how to make pancakes?"

"Woman, I was raised by a single dad with two kids. Of course I know how to make pancakes." I roll out of bed, already missing her warmth. "The question is, do you have actual food in your kitchen, or just coffee and whatever sad desk lunch you've been surviving on?"

"I have food," she protests, then pauses. "Okay, I have eggs. And milk and... is peanut butter food?"

I shake my head in mock disappointment. "City girl. Good thing I stopped at the store yesterday."

Her eyebrows shoot up. "You went grocery shopping? When? Where is this food?"

"Before I came here." I shrug. "It's in the pack on my bike. Wanted to make sure we had something for breakfast. Just in case."

The look she gives me could power the entire town. Soft and amazed and tender in a way that makes my chest tight.

"Lee Armstrong," she says quietly. "You bought me groceries."

"It's just premix pancake batter."

"You bought me groceries because you were hoping I'd let you spend the night." She sits up, the sheet pooling around her waist. "That might be the sweetest thing anyone's ever done for me."

"It's just food, Kya."

She shakes her head, but she's smiling.

I roll my eyes, ruffle her hair and roll out of bed. "Coffee first or shower?"

"Shower," she says immediately. "Followed immediately by coffee. I'm not human until I've had coffee."

"Noted. One cup of humanity, coming up."

I dress and head outside to retrieve the pancake mix and syrup from my saddlebags before coming back in to start her ancient coffee maker. The thing gurgles and protests but eventually produces something that smells like coffee.

I hear the shower start, and despite my best intentions, my mind immediately goes to places it shouldn't. Kya naked, water running down those curves I've been trying not to think about, soap slicking over skin I'm dying to touch.

"Lee?" Her voice drifts from the bathroom, and I nearly drop the coffee pot.

"Yeah?"

"Can you come here for minute?"

My mouth goes dry.

Fuck. She's going to kill me.

I find myself walking toward the bathroom before I can think better of it. The door is cracked open, steam curling out, and through the frosted glass I can see her silhouette.

"What do you need?" I ask, my voice rougher than intended.

"Come in, please."

I step inside, and sweet hell, the sight nearly brings me to my knees. The shower door is clear enough that I can see everything—the water cascading down her body, her hands moving over her skin as she washes. She's a goddess, all soft curves and golden skin, and she knows exactly what she's doing to me.

"Think I'm clean enough?" she asks, running her hands through her hair, arching her back in a way that makes me bite back a groan.

"Not at all, filthy girl."

She chuckles and turns to face me fully, water running in rivulets down her breasts, and I grip the doorframe to keep myself upright. When her hands move lower, soaping her stomach, her thighs, I stop breathing entirely.

"Kya..."

"What?" she asks innocently, though her eyes are dark with heat.

When her hand slips between her legs, her head falls back against the tile with a soft moan, and I lose the last thread of my control. My own hand moves to my jeans, working the zipper down, because if she's going to torture me, I'm sure as hell not going through it alone.

We watch each other through the steam. The sound of water mingles with our ragged breathing.

Her fingers are slow, teasing. She's not desperate enough for my liking.

"You're a tease, aren't you, Kya?" I rasp, hand wrapped tight around my cock. "Let me see how pretty you look when you touch yourself."

Her breath stutters. Her eyes flick to mine, wide and wanting.

"You enjoy teasing me, sweetheart?" I murmur. "Right there, with your fingers buried in that sweet little pussy?"

She moans, hips rocking into her hand.

"Good girl," I groan, fisting my cock. "Fuck, look at you. So fucking wet for me. So greedy. You want me to watch you fall apart, don't you?"

She nods, eyes half-lidded, lips parting with another shaky gasp. Her free hand braces against the tile, her movements turning frantic.

"You're perfect, Kya. So fucking beautiful. You don't even know what you do to me," I grit out, stroking harder. "You were made to be worshipped. You hear me?"

"Lee…" she gasps, fingers trembling. "I'm—"

"Let go, baby. That's it. Let me hear you say my name when you come. Let me hear what mine sounds like from that pretty little mouth."

She cries out, loud and unrestrained, my name ripped from her throat. And that's all it takes. My vision blurs, my body tenses, and I come hard, thick stripes of release spilling over my hand, hips jerking as I grunt her name.

The steam clings to the air, heavy and silent.

Her chest heaves. So does mine.

She leans her forehead against the glass, eyes glazed, lips swollen. And I swear to god, if she lets me in there, I'll spend the next hour on my knees showing her what real fucking devotion feels like.

She reaches behind her and flicks the tap off.

"Best shower ever," she says breathlessly as she steps out, wrapping herself in a towel.

"We're going to be the death of each other," I mutter, adjusting my jeans.

"Probably. But what a way to go."

By the time we've both recovered, the coffee maker has finished gurgling, and the pancake batter is waiting.

Kya shuffles in just as I'm flipping the first batch of pancakes, now wearing an oversized sweater that hits mid-thigh and fuzzy socks. Her hair is damp, but she's brushed her teeth. I can tell because she's not covering her mouth anymore.

"You're actually making pancakes," she says, cupping the coffee I hand her.

"I'm a man of my word." I slide a perfect golden pancake onto a plate and hand it to her. "Syrup?"

"Yes please." She takes a long, reverent sip of the coffee, and I watch her shoulders relax, her eyes flutter closed, and what can only be described as a moan of pure satisfaction escape her lips.

"Better?" I ask, trying not to think about how that sound affects me.

"Marginally human now," she admits, taking another sip. "Give me five more minutes and I might even be pleasant company."

I flip another pancake, grinning. "I like grumpy Kya. She's adorable."

"You say that now, but be warned. Grumpy Kya is a menace to society."

"I agree. Calling me into that bathroom was diabolical." I stack pancakes on her plate, adding syrup and a pat of butter. "Eat. You're too skinny."

She raises an eyebrow. "Excuse me?"

"You heard me. When's the last time you had a proper breakfast? And don't say coffee counts."

She's quiet for a moment, cutting into her pancakes. "I don't really... eat breakfast usually. Coffee and maybe a granola bar if I remember."

"Jesus, Kya." I lean against the counter, studying her. "You run a bar, work fourteen-hour days, and survive on coffee and granola bars?"

"I've been busy—"

"You've been neglecting yourself," I correct. "Good thing you've got me now."

She breathes out a long sigh, ducking her head as she slices into another piece of pancake. "Thank you. It's nice having someone looking out for me."

"No problem."

She leans back in her chair, studying me with those sharp hazel eyes. "What's your day look like?"

"Church at 10."

"Church?"

"Club meeting," I explain, glancing at the clock. "You?"

"Opening the bar at eleven. Mercy's handling the lunch rush so I can catch up on paperwork." She wrinkles her nose. "The glamorous life of a business owner."

"Need help with anything? I could swing by after church."

"Trying to find excuses to see me already, Armstrong?"

"Always," I say without hesitation, making her blush. "But I'm also serious. Heavy lifting, intimidating suppliers, looking pretty. I'm good at all of it."

She laughs. "I might take you up on that."

I stand to clear our plates, but she catches my wrist. "Lee?"

"Yeah?"

"Last night... this morning... all of it. Thank you."

"For what?"

"For making me feel..." She trails off.

I wait while she searches for the words she needs.

"Taken care of," she says quietly. "It's nice."

The admission hits me right in the chest. I set down the plates and turn to face her fully, cupping her face in my hands.

"Get used to it," I say, brushing my thumb over her cheek. "I plan on taking care of you for a long time."

Before she can respond, I press her back against the refrigerator and kiss her. Really kiss her, deep and thorough and claiming. She melts into me with a soft sound that makes me want to forget about church and spend the day learning every sound she can make.

Fucking hell. I've never wanted to shirk my duty before.

When we break apart, we're both breathing hard.

"You could have had this earlier," I say against her lips. "But you made me wait."

She laughs, breathless. "But it's so much better without morning breath."

With a growl, I spin us around, lifting her easily onto the kitchen counter so we're at eye level. Her legs wrap around my waist automatically, and I settle between them like I belong there.

"Hi," I murmur, tucking a strand of hair behind her ear.

"Hi yourself."

I kiss her again, softer this time but no less intense. When I pull back, she's looking at me with an expression I can't quite read.

"What?" I ask.

"We've already done three things," she says, smiling.

"Three things?"

"From our list last night. Morning coffee together, kissing against the fridge, and..." She gestures between us. "Now the counter."

"Guess we're overachievers," I say, catching her mouth for another slow, lingering kiss.

"Guess so," she murmurs when I finally draw back.

I check the time on my phone and curse under my breath. "I need to go. Church starts in an hour and I have some shit I need to get done."

"Go," she says, but her arms tighten around my neck. "Come hang out with me at the bar tonight?"

"That I can do." I kiss her one more time, quick and hard, then force myself to step back. "I'll text you after church."

"I'll be waiting."

I grab my helmet and cut, pausing at the door to look back at her. She's still sitting on the counter, hair wild, lips swollen from my kisses, looking thoroughly debauched and absolutely beautiful.

"Kya?"

"Yeah?"

"Best fucking night of my life."

Her smile could stop traffic. "Mine too."

I walk backward down her garden path. "And just think. I haven't even fucked you yet."

I grin as she throws back her head and laughs.

The ride to the clubhouse should take less than ten minutes, but I stretch it to forty, taking the long way through the hills outside town. I need space to get my head right.

By the time I pull into the lot behind the clubhouse, most of the bikes are already there. Church starts at ten sharp, and it's 9:55. I'm cutting it close, but that's nothing new.

I push through the back door and head straight for the chapel, grabbing coffee from the machine in the hallway. The room is already full, voices low and serious as the brothers settle into their usual spots around the scarred wooden table.

Stone glances up when I enter, his eyes taking in my appearance with the practiced assessment of a father who's been reading his children's moods for decades. There's a small flaw in my plan to keep what's going on with Kya quiet —I'm wearing the same clothes as yesterday.

Fuck.

"Cutting it close, son," he says mildly.

"Slept late," I lie, sliding into my usual seat between Bones and Cash.

Bones gives me a once-over and grins. "Rough night?"

"Something like that," I mutter, taking a sip of coffee that tastes like motor oil.

"Alright, let's get started," Stone says, rapping his knuckles on the table. "Church is in session."

The next hour is standard business—security updates, upcoming runs, a dispute between two prospects that needs settling. I contribute when necessary, but my mind keeps drifting to this morning. To Kya's sleepy smile, her teasing, the way she tasted, the sound she made when I—

"Which brings us to the Summit situation," Stone says, interrupting my thoughts. "Any updates?"

Hawk straightens in his chair. "They've been quiet since their visit to Devil's. My gut says they're planning something bigger."

"What about the lawyer?" Duck asks. "Josie making any progress?"

"Some. She's filed the preliminary injunctions to block the zoning changes, but it's a slow process. Could take months to get a hearing."

"We don't have months," Axel says grimly. "The count was finalized last night. They managed to secure two of the three seats they were chasing."

There are curses from around the table.

"We'll deal with it," I say, speaking up for the first time. "Whatever it takes."

Stone's eyes find mine across the table. "You've been hanging around Devil's. Any news?"

There's something in his tone. It's not quite teasing, but close. A few of the brothers exchange glances, and I realize I've walked right into whatever this is.

"Nothing I haven't already shared," I say carefully.

"And yet it warrants closer scrutiny?" Duck asks, but the old bastard is grinning at me.

The fucker.

"Devil's is important to the community," I say, crossing my arms over my chest, determined not to be drawn into their fucking nonsense.

"Sure it is," Cash says with a grin. "And I'm sure your sudden interest has nothing to do with the hot new owner."

Shit.

"You fuckers done with your teasing? Or can we get back to business?"

Hawk snorts. "Not a chance. You gave me and Axel shit for weeks, it's time to eat your own medicine."

"I did not—" I start, then catch myself. I did. I absolutely did. *Damn it.*

"You know the new waitress at Devil's—Mercy? Well, she and I got to talking last night and it seems our man here had a little meet up with Kya at her house last night." Cash wiggles his eyebrows suggestively. "Wanna share with the group, hot stuff?"

The room erupts in laughter and catcalls. Bones claps me on the back hard enough to rattle my teeth, while Duck mutters something about "about damn time" under his breath.

"This is ridiculous," I protest, but no one's listening.

Cash holds up his hand, quieting the table once more. "And," he says, placing a hand on his chest dramatically, "it appears that our man here chose not to seal the deal. Mercy sent me a text just now. It seems Kya and Lee are taking it slow."

This predictably unleashes a new round of ribbing. I shake my head, letting them get this nonsense out of their system. Unfortunately for me, it seems Cash came prepared for this conversation.

He stands, holding up his phone. "Starting a pool," he announces. "Taking bets on how long it takes before Lee and Kya—"

"Don't you fucking dare," I warn.

"—get horizontal," he finishes with a grin.

"I want in," Bones says immediately, reaching for his wallet. "Twenty says they don't make it through the week."

"You're all insane," I say, but Duck is already nodding thoughtfully.

"I'll take two weeks," he says. "Boy's stubborn, but he's not stupid."

"Five days," Axel chimes in. "That woman's got him tied in knots. He won't last longer than that."

"I'm sitting right here," I point out.

"Three days," Hawk says quietly, and everyone turns to stare at him. He shrugs. "What? Have you seen her? She's his type to a fucking T."

The betting escalates quickly, with brothers calling out timeframes and amounts while Cash frantically scribbles notes in his phone. Even some of the prospects get in on the action, pooling their limited funds for longer odds.

"You getting in on this?" I say to Stone, who's watching the chaos with barely concealed amusement.

He grins. "I already did."

"Fucking hell. Betrayed by my own flesh and blood. It's creepy, you know, betting on this shit."

Stone just grins.

He lets the ribbing go on for another minute or so before calling for order.

"Alright, alright, you dicks. That's enough. We've got actual business to finish."

But the damage is done. For the rest of church, I catch brothers grinning at me and making not-so-subtle comments about "taking care of business" and "sealing the deal." By the time we're dismissed, I'm ready to punch someone.

"Don't look so sour," Bones says as we file out of the chapel. "It's nice to see you happy for once."

"I'm always happy," I protest.

"You're always content," he corrects. "There's a difference. And whatever's happening with you and Kya? It's good for you, brother. We're happy for you."

"You guys got a weird way of showing it," I say finally.

He claps me on the shoulder. "Now, appreciate if you could hold yourself together for another twenty-four hours. I got three hundred riding on you."

I flip him off and head for my bike, but I'm smiling despite myself. Because for all their teasing and inappropriate betting habits, the brothers are right about one thing.

I am happy. Happier than I've been in years.

And if that means dealing with a few crude jokes and losing bets, it's a small price to pay for whatever this thing with Kya might become.

My phone buzzes as I'm putting on my helmet.

UNKNOWN

Tell your girlfriend to sell.

The good mood evaporates instantly, replaced by cold, focused rage.

Summit.

I screenshot the message and send it to Stone, then start my bike.

They want to play games? Threaten Kya?

Fine. But they picked the wrong fight with the wrong man.

They're going to learn exactly why crossing the Stoneheart MC is the last mistake they'll ever make.

13

KYA

The afternoon crowd is steady but manageable when Lee walks through the front door just after four. I'm restocking glasses behind the bar when I see him, and my pulse does that annoying skip it's been doing every time I think about this morning.

He approaches the bar with purpose, his expression somewhere between amused and exasperated. Before I can ask what's wrong, he reaches across the bar, cups the back of my neck, and pulls me into a kiss that's thorough enough to make my toes curl.

"Hi," he murmurs against my lips when he finally pulls back.

"Hi yourself," I manage, slightly breathless. "What was that for?"

"Missed you," he says simply, then his expression shifts. "Also, we need to talk. Privately."

"Everything okay?"

"Define okay." He glances around the bar, noting the handful of customers scattered at various tables. "Office?"

I nod. Once the door is closed, he pulls out his phone.

"Got this after church," he says, handing it to me.

On the screen is a text from an unknown number.

UNKNOWN

Tell your girlfriend to sell.

My blood runs cold. "Summit?"

"Has to be." His jaw is tight. "They're escalating."

I stare at the message, my hands trembling slightly. "How do they even know about us?"

"Small town. Or they've been watching." His voice is hard, dangerous. "Either way, they're making it clear they can reach you through me."

"It's just a text," I say, but my voice sounds shaky even to my ears.

"It's a threat, Kya." He takes the phone back, his knuckles white as he grips it. "They know where I was last night, they know we're together, and they're showing they don't give a shit about your being with a club member."

I lean against my desk, processing this. "What do we do?"

"You don't do anything. This is something the club will handle."

I want to argue, but this is becoming a situation that's way outside my control.

"I need you to promise me something," Lee says, his gaze holding mine.

"What?"

"You don't go anywhere alone. Not until we figure out how serious they are."

I bristle at the suggestion. "Lee, I can't live in fear—"

"I'm not asking you to live in fear. I'm asking you to be smart." He steps closer, his hands settling on my hips. "Please, Kya. Just until we know what we're dealing with."

The concern breaks down my defenses. "Okay. But I'm not selling the bar."

"I wouldn't expect you to." He presses a quick kiss to my forehead. "We'll figure this out."

We head back to the main bar, where Mercy is wiping down tables and chatting with a customer. She looks up when we emerge, and I can see the questions in her eyes.

"Everything okay?" she asks when the customer leaves.

"Club stuff," Lee says, which isn't exactly a lie.

Before anyone can probe further, the front door opens and Cash walks in. He spots Lee immediately, and his expression shifts to something mischievous.

"Well, well," he says, sliding onto a barstool. "Look who couldn't stay away."

"Shut up," Lee mutters, but there's no real heat in it.

Cash orders a beer, then turns to me with barely contained glee. "Have you told him yet?"

"Not yet."

Lee's eyes narrow and he glances between me and Cash. "Told me what?"

I clear my throat. "Mercy told me about the sex bet. I thought it only fair, since your club's getting in on the action, that we should too."

Cash is practically vibrating with amusement. "She's placing her own bet."

"Seriously?"

"Why not?" I shrug. "If you idiots are going to profit off my personal business, I might as well get a piece of the action."

Lee looks like he's caught between amusement and horror. "You're okay with this?"

I grin. "We're going to do it anyway. Might as well get something out of it."

I pull some notes from my pocket and hand them over to Cash.

"Definitely feels like you're rigging the system. I approve," he says, tucking the bills into his wallet.

"All's fair in love and gambling," Mercy says cheerfully.

"What day did you pick?" Lee asks, and there's something dangerous in his voice.

I meet his gaze steadily. "The 17th."

"The 17th," he repeats slowly.

"That's two weeks away," Cash points out helpfully. "A long time when you're hot to trot."

"I'm aware," Lee says, his eyes never leaving mine.

"You're really going to make the man wait two weeks?" Mercy asks, shaking her head. "That's just cruel."

"Good things come to those who wait," I say primly.

Lee leans in, his jaw clenching. "You really wanna wait that long?"

No.

"We can do it," I say, faking a confidence I don't have.

Mercy whistles low. "You're both far braver than me. I saw the kiss he laid on you when he got here. Ain't no way I'd be waiting that long."

Cash chuckles then drains his beer and tosses money on the bar. "Good luck, you two. Try not to burn the place down."

After he leaves, Mercy makes herself scarce, muttering something about checking inventory in the back.

"Two weeks," Lee says again, moving around the bar until he's standing close enough that I can feel his body heat.

"Don't think we can make it?" I ask.

"If we do, it'll be through sheer willpower alone." He steps closer, backing me against the bar. His hands settle on either side of me, caging me in. "Because two weeks is a long time, Kya. And I want you. Bad."

I lift my chin, meeting his challenge. "We can do it. I believe in us."

His smile is slow, wicked. "Oh, I know we can. But just be aware, you'll be spending the next week in bed."

The promise in his voice sends heat pooling low in my belly, but I force myself to maintain eye contact. "Promises, promises."

"Don't believe me?" he murmurs, leaning down until his lips brush my ear. "I have two weeks to change your mind. And I intend to use every minute of it."

The shiver that runs through me is impossible to hide. When he pulls back, his smile is triumphant.

"Two weeks," he says one more time, then steps away, leaving me breathless and shaky against the bar.

"We'll see," I manage, but my voice comes out rougher than intended.

He grabs his cut from where he'd draped it over a chair, shrugging into it with fluid movements. "See you tomorrow, sweetheart."

After he leaves, I slump against the bar, my heart still racing. Mercy emerges from the back room, shaking her head.

"Girl, you are playing with fire."

"I know," I admit.

"You really think you can hold out for two weeks?"

I think about the way Lee looked at me, the promise in his voice, the heat in his eyes.

"Not at all."

14

LEE

The next morning, I'm up before dawn with a plan.

Kya needs 24-hour protection, and I happen to be between jobs while still flush after the last one, which happened to be for a high-profile, wealthy client. I can afford to take some time off.

I stop at the coffee cart on Main Street first, ordering her usual—medium dark roast, two sugars, splash of cream. The barista, a college kid named Tyler, knows the order by heart.

"The usual for Kya?" he asks, already reaching for a cup.

"That's the one."

He grins as he works. "You two are cute together. About time she had someone looking out for her."

I hand over a twenty for a four-dollar coffee. "Keep the change."

Devil's doesn't open until 11, but I know Kya's there early doing paperwork. Her car sits alone in the lot, and I can see lights on in the back office. Perfect.

I use the spare key she gave me yesterday and let myself in through the back door.

She's hunched over her laptop, blonde hair falling in waves around her face, wearing an oversized flannel. She looks up when she hears my footsteps, and the smile that spreads across her face hits me like a physical blow.

"Lee? What are you doing here so early?"

"Brought you coffee," I say, setting the cup on her desk. "Figured you could use the caffeine."

She reaches for it eagerly, wrapping both hands around the warm cup. "Thank you. I've been up since five trying to make sense of these supplier invoices."

"You're pushing yourself too hard."

She makes a noncommittal sound.

I run my fingers through her hair, working out the tangles. "You're going to burn yourself out at this rate."

"There's just so much to do. Devil didn't exactly have the best filing system. The invoices, the inventory, the staff schedules..." She trails off as my fingers find a particularly stubborn knot. "That feels good."

"I know." I keep working through her hair, massaging her scalp with gentle pressure. "What else needs doing?"

"The beer taps are acting up again. The walk-in cooler is

making a weird noise. And the front door still sticks. I should probably call a handyman, but—"

"I'll take care of it."

She pulls back to look at me. "Lee, you don't have to—"

"I want to." I tuck a strand of hair behind her ear, letting my fingers trail down her neck. "Let me help you, Kya. Let me take care of some of this stuff so you can focus on the important things."

"The bar is important—"

"The bar is important," I agree. "But so are you. And if you collapse from exhaustion, the bar doesn't matter."

She's quiet for a moment, studying my face. "Why?"

"Why what?"

"Why do you want to help? You don't owe me anything."

Her question catches me off guard. Not because I don't know the answer, but because the answer is bigger and more complicated than I'm ready to voice.

"Because I care about you," I say finally. "And watching you struggle when I can help makes me feel like a dick."

"Lee—"

"Shh." I press a soft kiss to the sensitive spot just below her ear, and she melts against me. "Let me fix your door. Let me look at the taps. Let me help."

"Okay," she whispers.

"Good." I press another kiss to her neck, this one with just a hint of teeth. "Good girl."

The praise makes her breath hitch, and I file that reaction away for later use.

The next two weeks are going to be hard, but fuck if they won't also be educational.

I spend the next hour fixing everything I can on her list and a few things that aren't. The door needed the hinges oiled. The kitchen taps required new washers, while the cooler needs a new gasket, which I order online and have expedited.

Kya's moved out to the bar to watch me work, sipping her coffee and pretending not to glance my way. But I catch her staring more than once, her eyes lingering on my hands, my shoulders. Her gaze feels like a warm touch across my back whenever I reach for something.

"Enjoying the show?" I ask when I catch her staring for the third time.

Pink floods her cheeks. "I don't know what you're talking about."

"Uh-huh." I finish tightening the last connection on the beer tap and test it. Perfect flow, no foam. "Try this."

I pour a small glass and hand it to her. She takes a sip, her eyes lighting up.

"That's so much better. How did you—"

"YouTube," I admit with a grin. I lean against the bar, watching her face. "What time does Mercy get in?"

"Ten-thirty. Why?"

I check my watch. Two hours. Perfect.

"Because I'm taking you to breakfast. Real breakfast. With actual food groups and everything."

"Lee, I have so much work—"

"The work will still be here when we get back. But you need to eat something that doesn't come out of a wrapper." I touch my foot to hers. "Don't make me throw you over my shoulder and carry you out of here."

"You wouldn't dare."

I lean in until my lips are almost touching hers. "Try me."

For a moment, I think she's going to keep arguing. Then her shoulders sag in defeat. "But we have to be back before the lunch start. I really do have a lot to do."

"Deal. Come on," I say, grabbing my cut from the chair. "We're taking a ride."

She stares at my outstretched hand for a moment, then sighs and takes it. "If I freeze to death on your bike, I'm haunting you."

"I've got an extra jacket in my saddlebag. You'll be fine." I reach into the other bag and pull out a second helmet, a sleek black model with silver trim. "And this."

Kya stares at the helmet in my hands. "You bought me a helmet?"

"Safety first," I say, though we both know it's more than that. "Can't have you riding around with some beat-up loaner. This one's yours."

She takes it carefully, running her fingers over the smooth surface. "Lee..."

"Just try it on."

She does, and it fits perfectly. Of course it does, I spent twenty minutes at the shop making sure I got the right size.

"How did you know what size to get?"

"Lucky guess," I lie. The truth is I'd asked Emma years ago, back when I thought I might get Kya on my bike someday. Never thought it would actually happen.

Twenty minutes later, we're climbing into the mountains on the winding road that leads to the peak. Kya's arms are wrapped around my waist, her body pressed against my back, and every curve makes her hold me tighter. It's torture of the best kind.

The ride up takes forty-five minutes, but there's a little place called Mountain View Café that sits right on the ridge. Family-owned, been there for decades, and they serve the kind of breakfast that'll stick to your ribs.

We pull into the gravel parking lot, and Kya climbs off the bike with shaky legs.

"That was..." She pauses, pulling off the helmet I'd given her. "Actually kind of amazing."

"Good. We'll have to do it more often." I lead her toward the weathered wooden building with its wraparound porch and mountain views. "Wait until you see the inside."

The café is exactly what you'd expect—checkered tablecloths, mismatched chairs, and windows that showcase the valley spreading out below us. We grab a table by the window, and I watch Kya take in the view.

"This is beautiful," she breathes. "I'd forgotten how gorgeous it is up here."

"Worth the ride?"

"Definitely." She picks up the menu, scanning it with renewed interest.

"The waffles here are supposed to be incredible," I tell her. "And the hash browns are basically a religious experience."

When the waitress comes, I order for both of us—waffles, eggs, bacon, hash browns, orange juice, and coffee. Enough food for three people, but I want Kya to have options. I want her to remember what it feels like to have abundance instead of scarcity.

"This is too much food," she protests when the plates arrive.

"Eat what you want. Take the rest home." I cut into my waffle, watching her do the same. "Tell me about Portland."

"What about it?"

"Your life there. What you liked about it. What you didn't."

She chews thoughtfully. "I liked the anonymity, I guess. No one knew my history or my family. I could be whoever I wanted to be."

"And who did you want to be?"

"Someone who had her shit together. Someone successful and independent and..." She trails off, stabbing at her eggs. "Someone who didn't need anyone."

"Did it work?"

"For a while." She takes another bite, and I'm gratified to see her actually enjoying the food. "But it was lonely. I had work friends, but no one I could call if I had a bad day, you know? No one who really knew me."

"You could have called Emma."

"Could I?" She looks up at me. "Emma's living her dream in New York. She's got this amazing career, this perfect life. The last thing she needs is her old best friend calling to complain about her problems."

"That's not how friendship works, Kya. Real friends want to be there for the bad stuff too."

"Maybe." She doesn't sound convinced.

I reach across the table to steal her hand, raising it to my lips. The kiss is barely there, just a brush of my mouth against her knuckles, but she inhales sharply. I do it again, this time with the barest hint of tongue, and watch her pupils dilate.

"Lee—"

"Eat your breakfast, sweetheart." I release her hand and return to my own food. "We should get back soon."

She stares at me for a moment, clearly trying to process what just happened. Then she shakes her head and picks up her fork, but I catch the slight tremor in her hands.

Good. Let her think about that kiss, about the promise in it. Let her wonder what else I'm planning.

By the time we get back to Devil's, Mercy's car is in the lot. We find her setting up the bar, humming along to whatever's playing on the jukebox.

"Well, well," she says when she sees us. "Look at what the cat dragged in."

"Good morning to you too," Kya says, poking her tongue out at her.

I stay to help set up for the lunch rush, but as they open the doors, my phone buzzes with a text.

STONE

Church at 2. Urgent.

I show Kya the message. "I have to go. Club business."

"Everything okay?"

"Probably just routine stuff." I lean in, pressing a quick kiss to her cheek. "Call me if you need anything. And eat some actual lunch."

"I will."

I start to leave, then turn back. "Kya?"

"Yeah?"

"I'll be here before close. And if I can't get here, a prospect will. I don't want you alone, got me?"

She bites her lip. "Lee, you don't have to—"

"I want to." I meet her gaze steadily. "Let me take care of you."

"Okay," she says softly.

"Good." I flash her a grin. "And note, I'll be bringing an overnight bag."

She narrows her eyes. "And you'll be sleeping on the couch, sir. I have a bet to win."

The clubhouse is buzzing with activity when I arrive. Brothers clustered in small groups, voices low and serious. Whatever this is about, it's big.

Stone calls the meeting to order, and we file into the chapel. The atmosphere is tense, focused in a way that usually means trouble.

"Josie has a friend on the council who dropped us some intel," Stone begins without preamble. "And it's bad news."

Hawk spreads a map on the table. Red X's mark various properties throughout downtown, with arrows indicating planned developments.

"They want the entire historic district," Hawk explains. "Eight blocks, including the residential neighborhoods on Oak Street and Pine Avenue."

My blood runs cold. Oak Street is where Duck lives with his wife. Pine Avenue is home to half a dozen club families, people who've been part of this community for generations.

"What's their timeline?" Axel asks.

"Fast," Stone replies grimly. "They've already got the council votes they need for the commercial rezoning. Residential is next on the agenda in two months."

"And if they pass the changes?"

"Everyone in those neighborhoods gets bought out or forced out. Historic homes get torn down for condos and strip malls." Stone's jaw is tight. "They're trying to erase the soul of this town."

Cash leans forward. "What's Josie say about this?"

"She's working on it, but legal challenges take time. Time we might not have."

"So what's the play?" I ask.

"I want everyone reaching out to their contacts," Stone continues. "Property owners, businesspeople, anyone with influence. If we can prevent Devil's being rezoned, we might have a fighting chance with the other areas."

"What about the townsfolk?" Duck asks. "If these bastards are willing to threaten Kya over one bar, what happens when we start pushing back?"

"We protect our own," Stone says simply. "And anyone else who stands with us."

The meeting continues for another hour, assignments handed out, strategies discussed. By the time we're dismissed, everyone knows their role in the coming fight.

But as I head back to my bike, my thoughts aren't on Summit or strategy. They're on Kya, alone at the bar, unaware that the threat just got exponentially bigger.

I pull out my phone and send her a text.

LEE

How's your day going?

Her response comes back almost immediately.

KYA

Good. Mercy's handling things beautifully.
Looking forward to seeing you.

The simple message makes me smile despite everything. Whatever's coming, whatever Summit has planned, I'll be damned if I let them touch her.

Tonight, I'll make her laugh, make her feel safe, make her forget about everything except us.

And then I'll spend the next thirteen days driving her absolutely wild.

Two can play this game, Kya Sullivan. But only one of us is going to win.

15

KYA

Four days into Lee's campaign to drive me insane, I'm ready to throw in the towel.

He's on my couch, takeout containers scattered across the coffee table, looking completely at home in my space. He's changed out of his cut into gray sweatpants and a white T-shirt that clings to every muscle.

If men had a slutty clothing equivalent, this would be it.

"You're staring," he says without looking up from his lo mein.

"I'm appreciating," I correct, taking another bite of my orange chicken.

"There's a difference?" He glances up, that dangerous smile playing at the corners of his mouth. "And what exactly are you appreciating?"

The way your shirt stretches across your chest. The way your throat moves when you swallow. The way you've been slowly, methodically driving me out of my mind for four straight days...

"Your chopstick skills," I lie.

He snorts. "Really? That's the bet you can come up with?"

"It's the truth."

"Uh-huh." He sets down his container and shifts on the couch, angling his body toward mine. "Come here."

"I'm perfectly fine where I am, thank you."

"Kya." His voice drops to that low, commanding tone that makes my stomach flip. "Come here."

I should resist. I should stay exactly where I am, finish my dinner, and then go straight to bed. Instead, I find myself setting down my food and sliding across the couch until I'm close enough to feel his body heat.

"That's better," he murmurs, his arm coming around me to pull me against his side.

I fit perfectly there, my head on his shoulder, my hand resting on his chest. I can feel his heartbeat under my palm, steady and strong, and it takes everything I have not to trail my fingers lower.

"How was your day?" he asks, his fingers playing with my hair.

"Quiet. A few regulars, some paperwork. Nothing exciting." I tilt my head to look at him. "What about you? More club stuff?"

His expression darkens slightly. "Just keeping an eye on things. Making sure Summit doesn't try anything else."

"They've been quiet since that text."

"For now." His fingers tighten in my hair, just enough to make me shiver. "But quiet doesn't mean gone."

I don't want to think about Summit right now. I don't want to think about threats or danger or anything that exists outside this moment, with Lee's arm around me and his fingers in my hair.

"Lee?"

"Yeah?"

"I'm glad you're here."

"How glad?"

Our kiss is soft at first, but it quickly heats up. I lose myself in the feel of his mouth, the way his tongue slides against mine, the soft sound he makes when I thread my fingers through his hair. This is what I've been craving for days, this connection, this heat, this feeling like I might actually die if he stops touching me.

His hands are everywhere—my face, my hair, sliding down to grip my waist and pull me closer. I end up in his lap somehow, straddling his thighs, my chest pressed against his as we kiss like we're drowning and this is our only source of air.

"Fuck," he breathes against my lips. "Kya—"

"Don't stop," I whisper, grinding down against him just enough to feel how hard he is through his jeans. "Please don't stop."

His hands fist in my shirt, holding me still. "The bet—"

"I know." I kiss along his jaw, tasting salt and something uniquely him. "I know, but just... We could lie..."

"You want to lie?" His voice is strained, like he's barely holding on to his control.

"Just touch me. Please. I need... I need *something*."

For a moment, I think he's going to say no.

Instead, he says, "Fuck it," and his mouth is on my neck, hot and hungry.

I gasp as he finds that sensitive spot just below my ear. His hands slide under my shirt, palms hot against my skin, and I arch into his touch.

"Is this okay?" he asks against my throat.

"More than okay," I manage, tugging at his shirt. "Take this off."

He pulls back just long enough to drag his shirt over his head, and I have to bite back a moan at the sight of him. Broad shoulders, defined chest, abs that look like they were carved from stone. But it's the stories written on his skin that steal my breath.

A military tattoo covers his left shoulder surrounded by dates I know must mark deployments. Below it, script in another language winds around his ribs. There's the Stoneheart MC logo across his right pec, and a jagged scar along his collarbone that looks like it came from a knife. Another smaller one marks his hip that's too precise to be anything but a bullet wound.

This is what his life has been, violence and danger and

missions I can't even imagine. The evidence is carved into his skin, permanent reminders of how volatile his world is.

I run my hands over his chest, feeling the way his muscles jump under my palms, tracing the raised edges of scars that could have taken him from me before I ever had the chance to have him. He's warm and solid and perfect, and I want to map every inch of him with my mouth.

"Your turn," he says, his hands already working at the hem of my shirt.

I let him pull it off, suddenly self-conscious as his gaze travels over my body. I'm not wearing anything special, just a simple black bra that's more functional than sexy, but the way he looks at me makes me feel like I'm wearing the most beautiful lingerie in the world.

"Jesus," he breathes. "You're fucking gorgeous."

Before I can respond, he's kissing me again, deeper this time, his hands skimming over my bare skin like he's memorizing every curve. When his thumb brushes over my nipple through the thin fabric of my bra, I cry out, the sound swallowed by his mouth.

"Sensitive," he murmurs against my lips, doing it again just to hear me make that sound.

"Lee—"

"I know, baby. I know." His hands are at my back, working at the clasp of my bra. "Let me see you."

The bra falls away, and I should feel exposed, vulnerable. Instead, I feel powerful, desired, beautiful under his hungry gaze.

"Perfect," he says, his voice rough with want. "Absolutely fucking perfect."

Then his mouth is on me, hot and wet and perfect, and I lose all ability to think coherently. All I can do is arch into him, my hands fisted in his hair, as he worships my body with a devotion that makes my heart ache.

"I want more," I gasp when he switches his attention to my other breast. "Lee, please—"

"What do you want?" he asks, pulling back to look at me. His eyes are dark, pupils blown wide with desire. "Tell me what you need."

"You," I whisper. "I need you."

Something shifts in his expression, becomes more intense, more focused. "Lean back."

I do as he says, settling back against the arm of the couch, and watch as he slides down my body. His hands are at the waistband of my leggings, fingers hooking under the elastic.

"These need to come off," he says, already starting to work them down my legs.

"Lee, we said—"

"We said no sex," he interrupts, pulling my leggings off completely and tossing them aside. "This isn't sex."

My underwear is next, black cotton that he removes with one swift jerk down my legs. And then I'm naked on my couch, Lee kneeling between my thighs, looking at me like I'm something holy.

"Beautiful," he murmurs, his hands stroking up my thighs. "So fucking beautiful."

"Lee—"

"Shh." His thumbs brush over my hip bones, making me shiver. "Let me take care of you, baby. Let me make you feel good."

And then his mouth is on me. And my world *shatters*.

Lee licks me like he's starving and has finally allowed himself to feast. His tongue flicks over my clit in firm, devastating strokes, dragging a gasp from my lips before I can even think.

"Oh fuck," I cry, hips jerking as pleasure ignites low in my belly.

He growls against me, the sound sending vibrations through every nerve ending. "You taste like sin, baby. I could die between these thighs."

His grip tightens on my hips, holding me down as I writhe beneath him. One hand slides up to splay over my stomach, pinning me open, *claiming* me. I'm exposed, vulnerable. And I love it.

"Lee—oh my god!"

"That's it," he murmurs, dragging his tongue flat and slow before teasing my clit again. "Let me make you come."

He circles my clit, then sucks—*hard*—and I arch off the couch with a strangled cry.

"Good girl."

He doesn't rush. Doesn't let up. He flicks, sucks, licks, all in an effort to get me off. Every sound I make just urges him on, until I'm panting, begging, hips rolling helplessly under his tongue.

"Please," I sob. "Please, Lee—"

"What do you need, sweetheart?" His breath is hot, teasing. "Want me to lick some more? Want me to suck on this perfect little clit until you lose your fucking mind? Do you need some fingers to fill you up, sweetheart?"

"Yes! Yes—please, please."

His fingers thrust inside me, slow and obscene, while his mouth presses perfectly to my clit. I can feel everything tightening, spiraling, winding higher—

I'm shaking. Gasping.

Teetering.

"Come for me," he commands. "Right fucking *now*."

That's all it takes.

The orgasm hits like a tidal wave—violent, endless, all-consuming. I cry out, legs trembling, hands fisting in the couch cushions as he continues to devour me.

Even as I twitch and whimper and try to breathe again, he's licking up every drop.

I can't speak. Can't think.

I'm boneless. Drenched. Ruined.

It's not until I murmur a protest that he backs off, shifting to gently kiss my inner thigh and whisper praise against my flushed skin.

When I finally open my eyes, he's watching me with an expression of pure male satisfaction.

"Holy shit," I manage.

"Good?" he asks, though the smug smile on his face suggests he already knows the answer.

"Good is... that's not even close to the right word."

He chuckles, pressing one more kiss to my hip before sitting back on his heels.

I reach for him, wanting to return the favor, but he catches my hands.

"No," he says firmly.

"But you didn't—"

"This was for you." He brings my hands to his lips, pressing a kiss to each palm.

"That's not fair."

"Life's not fair, sweetheart." He stands, reaching for his shirt. "But the wait will be worth it. I promise."

I watch in disbelief as he pulls his shirt back on, like nothing happened. Like he didn't just give me the most intense orgasm of my life and then stop.

"You're really just going to... leave?"

"I'm going to go take a very cold shower," he says, leaning down to kiss my forehead. "And then we're going to bed.

And while you sleep, I'll no doubt lie beside you thinking about the sounds you just made and counting down the hours until I can taste your sweet cunt again."

"You're killing me," I groan, pulling a throw pillow over my face.

"Nine more days," he says, and I can hear the amusement in his voice. "Think you can handle it?"

I peek over the pillow to glare at him. "I hate you."

"No, you don't. You love that I have enough self-control for both of us."

"I really, really don't."

"Yes, you do. Because when we finally get to the 17th, you're going to be so desperate for me that you won't be able to see straight." He leans down one more time, his lips brushing my ear. "And I'm going to spend hours taking you apart, piece by piece, until you're screaming my name."

A shiver runs through me at the promise in his voice. "Lee—"

"Nine more days, baby. Think you can last that long?"

I want to say no. I want to tell him to forget the bet, forget everything, and take me to bed right now. But there's something in his eyes, a challenge and a promise all wrapped up together, that makes me bite back the words.

"We'll see," I manage.

"We will." He's headed for the shower before I can come up with a response, leaving me naked on my couch, boneless and satisfied and somehow more frustrated than ever.

Nine more days.

I'm never going to survive this.

16

LEE

The cold shower doesn't help.

Neither does the second one, or the third. By the time I give up and crawl into bed, I'm still hard enough to cut glass and wound tight enough to snap. The taste of Kya is still on my tongue, the sound of her coming apart under my mouth still echoing in my ears.

Nine more days of this is going to kill me. But fuck she isn't worth it.

I wake up to sunlight streaming through Kya's bedroom windows and the sound of her phone buzzing insistently on the nightstand. She stirs beside me, warm and soft under the blankets.

"Mmm," she mumbles, reaching blindly for the phone. "Hello?"

I can hear Mercy's voice, tinny and urgent through the speaker. "Kya, you need to get to the bar. Now."

That gets her attention. She sits up, the sheet pooling around her waist, and I have to force myself to focus on the conversation instead of the way the morning light plays across her skin.

"What's wrong?" she asks, instantly alert.

"Health inspectors. They showed up an hour ago with a warrant. County officials, the works. They're tearing the place apart."

Fuck.

I jerk up, already rolling out of bed.

"What?" Kya throws back the covers, reaching down to the floor with one hand to look for clothes. "How is that even legal? We don't open until—"

"They got a complaint. Multiple complaints, actually. Anonymous tips about serious health violations."

I tug on my jeans. "Summit," I mutter, and Kya nods grimly.

"We'll be there in ten minutes," she tells Mercy, hanging up.

"Make that seven," I say, already pulling my shirt on. "You're riding with me."

We make it to Devil's in five, my bike eating up the distance while Kya holds tight behind me. I can feel the tension in her body as we pull into the lot and see the official vehicles parked outside—a county health department van, two cop cars, and a black sedan that screams government bureaucrat.

Inside, it's chaos. A stern-faced woman in a county jacket is going through the kitchen with a fine-tooth comb while a uniformed officer stands nearby looking bored. Another inspector is examining the bar itself, taking photos and making notes on a tablet.

Mercy spots us first, relief flooding her face as we enter. "Thank God you're here," she says, hurrying over. "They've been at this for over an hour. They only just let me call you."

Kya moves behind the bar, her professional mask sliding into place as she surveys the damage. I stay close, positioning myself where I can see both her and the inspectors.

"Mr. Armstrong," a voice calls out, and I turn to see a man in an expensive suit approaching. He's older, silver-haired, with the kind of predatory smile that makes my skin crawl. "David Crane, Summit Development."

"And you're here why exactly?" I reply, stepping closer to the bar and Kya.

"Summit is the government's official contractor for health inspections in this county. I'm just here to oversee the investigation."

I grit my teeth. "And you just so happen to choose Devil's to examine?"

The bastard chuckles. "No, I'm afraid this isn't a routine check. We received several complaints about food safety violations at this establishment. The county takes these things very seriously."

Complaints, my ass. This is intimidation, pure and simple.

"Find anything interesting?" I ask, though I already know

the answer. Kya runs a tight ship—there's nothing for them to find.

"A few minor infractions," Crane says smoothly. "Improper food storage temperatures, some documentation issues. Nothing that can't be corrected with the proper guidance."

"Guidance from Summit Development?" Kya asks, her voice deceptively calm.

"From the appropriate regulatory agencies, of course. Though Summit would be happy to assist with any renovations or upgrades needed to bring the establishment into compliance."

"For a fee, I'm sure."

"Naturally. These things are expensive. Though perhaps less expensive than the alternative."

I take a step forward, and Crane's smile falters slightly. "What alternative would that be?"

"Closure, naturally. If the violations are severe enough, the county has no choice but to shut down non-compliant establishments until they meet standards."

Kya's face goes pale, but her voice remains steady. "And I suppose Summit would be willing to buy the property at a fair price? Help me avoid all this unpleasantness?"

"We're always interested in worthwhile investments," Crane agrees. "Our offer still stands, Ms. Sullivan. Perhaps we could discuss terms—"

"Perhaps you could get the fuck out of my bar," Kya interrupts, all pretense of politeness gone. "Unless you're planning to order something, you're not welcome here."

Crane's smile turns predatory. "Ms. Sullivan, I'd encourage you to reconsider your position. The county takes health violations very seriously. It would be unfortunate if this establishment were forced to close due to... ongoing compliance issues."

That's when I step between them, close enough that Crane has to crane his neck to look up at me. "Is that a threat?"

"Simply a statement of fact. Health codes exist for public safety. When establishments consistently fail to meet standards..." He shrugs.

The health inspector approaches, tablet in hand. "Ms. Sullivan? I need to speak with you about our findings."

Kya moves around the bar, and I follow close behind. The inspector—a no-nonsense woman in her fifties—pulls up a list on her tablet.

"Overall, the establishment is in good condition," she begins, and I see Crane's expression darken. "However, I did find a few minor violations. The walk-in cooler temperature log hasn't been updated in three days, and you're missing some documentation for your most recent supplier deliveries."

"That's it?" Kya asks.

"That's it. Both are easily correctable—just need updated logs and paperwork. I'll need to see the corrections within seven days. As this is your first infraction, we're issuing you with a formal warning to comply." She tears off a piece of paper. "I'll be back in a week to check over the improvements."

Kya's relief is palpable, and I catch Crane's frustrated scowl out of the corner of my eye.

"However," the inspector continues, "I should mention that my office has received several complaints in the past week. All anonymous, all claiming serious violations. I want to be clear—those complaints were baseless. This inspection found no evidence of the issues described."

"Anonymous complaints," Kya repeats.

"Yes. Which is unusual. In my experience, legitimate complaints usually come from identifiable sources. Anonymous ones are often…" She glances meaningfully at Crane. "Motivated by other concerns. I'd recommend reviewing the health standards with your staff to ensure you're compliant, just to be safe."

I grin. It seems that while she might be employed by Summit, the inspector isn't a fan of Crane either.

After the inspector leaves, along with the cops and the rest of the county officials, Crane lingers, his earlier confidence replaced by barely contained anger.

"This establishment sits on prime development real estate, Ms. Sullivan. One way or another, Summit will acquire it. The question is whether you'll choose to sell voluntarily or… find yourself with no other options."

"Get out," Kya says quietly. "Now."

I want to rip this weasel's fucking head off and use it as a paperweight. My anger bubbles over, every instinct screaming at me to put this piece of shit through the nearest wall. But Kya's handling this, and she's more than capable. I take a step closer to her, not interfering, just letting her know silently that I'm here if she needs me.

Crane doesn't move. Just stands there with that smug expression, clearly thinking he can intimidate her into submission.

That's when I step forward.

"The lady asked you to leave," I say, my voice deadly quiet. "I suggest you listen."

Crane's eyes flick to me, and whatever he sees in my expression makes him finally straighten his tie and head for the door. The man, for all his faults, isn't completely useless. He straightens his tie, smoothing his hand over his chest.

"Best of luck to you." He leaves, and the bar falls silent except for the hum of the refrigeration units and the distant sound of traffic outside.

"Well," Mercy says finally. "That was fun."

"Are you okay?" I ask Kya, noting the slight tremor in her hands.

"I'm fine. Just angry." She runs her hands through her hair, messing up the careful style. "They're not going to stop, are they?"

"No," I admit. "They're not."

"So what do we do?"

Before I can answer, the front door opens and Cash walks in, followed by Bones and three of the prospects. They take in the scene and their expressions harden.

"Heard there was some excitement," Cash says, settling at the bar.

"Summit brought the health department," I explain. "Harassment, pure and simple."

"Find anything?" Bones asks.

"Minor stuff. Nothing that can't be fixed in a day."

"But they'll be back," Kya adds grimly.

"Then we'll be ready for them," Cash says simply. "What do you need?"

It's a simple question, but the weight behind it is enormous. This is the club offering protection, resources, solidarity. Kya looks surprised by the immediate support.

"I don't—" she starts.

"Documentation," I interrupt. "Security cameras. Witnesses for every inspection. Make it harder for them to manufacture violations."

"Done," Bones says, already pulling out his phone. "Hawk can have cameras installed by tomorrow."

"What about legal support?" Mercy asks. "Isn't there a lawyer helping with the zoning stuff?"

"Josie Bright," I confirm. "She specializes in municipal law and corruption cases. She should know about this."

"I'll call her," Cash offers. "Pass on the info from today."

"And I'll talk to Stone about increasing patrols," I add. "Make sure there's always someone keeping an eye on things."

Kya looks overwhelmed by the sudden outpouring of support. "You don't have to—"

"Yes, we do," Bones interrupts gently. "You're one of us. We protect our own."

"But I'm not—"

"You are," I say firmly. "Whether you realize it or not, you're family. And family sticks together."

Tears shine in her eyes, but she blinks them back. "I feel like you should have said that in a Vin Diesel voice."

I huff, pulling her into me for a hug. "Just take the win, Kya."

She sniffles against my chest. "Okay. Thank you."

"Don't thank us yet," Cash says. "Wait until you see Hawk's bill for the security system."

That earns a laugh, breaking some of the tension.

"Feel better?" I ask Kya.

"A little. Still angry, but less... helpless, I guess." She tilts her head back. "Thank you. For coming with me when Mercy called, and for stepping in with Crane."

"You don't need to thank me for that."

"Yes, I do. It's my problem, my bar, my fight."

"It stopped being just your fight the minute they threatened you. You're mine, Kya." The words are rough. "Maybe we haven't said it out loud, maybe we're still figuring out what this is, but you're mine. And I protect what's mine."

Something flickers in her eyes—surprise, desire, something deeper that makes my chest tight.

"Yours," she repeats softly.

"Mine," I confirm, stepping closer until there's barely an inch between us. "The same way I'm yours."

She goes up on her toes, and I think she's going to kiss me. Instead, she presses her forehead against mine, breathing unsteadily.

"Eight more days," she whispers.

"Eight more days," I agree, even though every instinct I have is screaming at me to take her home and claim her properly.

"We should get to work."

"We should," I agree. Neither of us moves.

With a laugh, she finally steps back and twirls, walking away. My gaze drops to her full ass, appreciating the way it moves in her tight jeans.

Eight fucking days.

17

KYA

The health inspector finishes her review at exactly 4:47 p.m. on the 17th.

"Everything looks perfect, Ms. Sullivan," she says, signing off on the final paperwork with a satisfied nod. "Temperature logs are up to date, all documentation is in order, and the kitchen is spotless. Consider this matter closed."

I'm so relieved that my knees nearly buckle. "Thank you. Thank you so much."

"Just keep up the good work." She tucks her clipboard into her bag. "And between you and me? Those anonymous complaints were clearly harassment. I've filed a report with my supervisor about the suspicious timing and baseless nature of the original violations. I don't abide by vexatious claims."

After she leaves, I stand in the middle of Devil's and just breathe. Seven days of stress, of constantly looking over my shoulder, of checking and double-checking every detail. It's finally over.

Well, almost over.

I glance at the clock behind the bar, 4:52 p.m.

In just over seven hours, I'll win the bet.

In just over seven hours, Lee is going to make good on every single promise he's whispered in my ear over the past two weeks.

Heat pools low in my belly at the thought, and I have to grip the edge of a table to steady myself. These past few days have been absolute torture. Lee's campaign to drive me insane has been ruthlessly effective—lingering touches that set my skin on fire, heated looks that make me forget how to breathe, and a constant undercurrent of sexual tension that has me wound tighter than a spring.

Last night, he'd shown up at my cottage with dinner and spent two hours eating me out. When I'd tried to return the favor, he'd pinned my hands above my head and kissed me until I was dizzy, then walked away to have a cold shower.

"Twenty-nine more hours, sweetheart."

I'd nearly thrown a shoe at his head.

"Earth to Kya," Mercy says, snapping me out of my thoughts. "You okay? You look like you're about to spontaneously combust."

"I'm fine," I lie, straightening napkin dispensers that don't need straightening. "Just relieved about the inspection."

"Uh-huh." She leans against the bar, studying me with knowing eyes. "So that flush on your face has nothing to do with the fact that a certain tattooed biker has been eye-fucking you for two weeks?"

"Mercy—"

"Girl, the sexual tension between you two is so thick I could cut it with a knife. Half our customers have been placing side bets on whether you'll make it to midnight without jumping each other."

I stare at her. "There are side bets?"

"Honey, there are side bets on the side bets. Mrs. Henderson from the diner put fifty dollars on you caving before the dinner rush."

"Mrs. *Henderson* bet on my sex life?"

"She also brought homemade cookies and said to tell you that young love is beautiful and you should grab happiness with both hands." Mercy grins. "Direct quote."

I bury my face in my hands. "This town is insane."

"This town loves a good love story. And you and Lee? That's the kind of epic romance people write songs about."

Before I can respond, the front door opens and Lee walks in. He's wearing his cut over a simple white T-shirt and dark jeans, but the way he moves—all controlled power and lethal grace—makes my mouth go dry.

His eyes find mine immediately, and the heat in them is enough to melt steel.

"Ladies," he says, his voice rough in a way that sends shivers down my spine.

"Lee," Mercy replies cheerfully. "Just checking on our girl after her big victory."

"Victory?" He raises an eyebrow, though his gaze never leaves my face.

"Passed the health inspection with flying colors," I manage to say. "We're officially in the clear."

"I never had a doubt."

We grin at each other, and I want to reach out and touch him, but I know if I do, that bet is as sure as hell not going to be won.

"Well," Mercy says, clearly enjoying the show, "I think I'll go check inventory in the back. Take my time with it. Maybe count everything twice. Be super thorough. Might take me a while."

She disappears before either of us can respond, leaving Lee and me alone in the main bar area.

"Subtle," Lee says, rolling his eyes. "How are you feeling?"

"Good. Relieved. Ready for this whole Summit thing to be over."

"I wasn't talking about Summit."

Oh.

"Nervous," I admit. "Excited. Like I might die if you don't touch me soon."

His pupils dilate, and I watch his hands clench into fists at his sides. "Kya—"

"I know. Seven more hours." I check the clock, 5:15. "Six hours and forty-five minutes, actually."

"You're counting."

"Down to the second." I move around the bar, ostensibly to clean glasses, but really because I need something to do with my hands. "Are you counting?"

"Every fucking minute." His voice is strained. "Do you have any idea what these past two weeks have been like for me?"

I look up at him, noting the tight line of his jaw, the way his T-shirt stretches across his chest with each controlled breath. "Probably about the same as they've been for me."

"I doubt that." He leans against the bar, close enough that I can smell his cologne. "I've been taking cold showers three times a day and still going to bed rock hard."

Heat floods my cheeks. "Lee, I—"

"I've been dreaming about you every night. About the sounds you make when you come, about how you taste, about all the things I'm going to do to you when this bet is over."

My breath catches. "What things?"

His smile is pure sin. "You'll find out. Soon."

The next few hours pass in a haze of sexual tension so thick it's practically visible. Lee helps with the evening crowd, and every accidental touch—his hand brushing mine when he hands me a glass, his body pressed against my back when he reaches around me for something—sends electricity shooting through my nervous system.

By 9 p.m., I'm ready to climb the walls.

By 9.30 p.m., I'm seriously considering forfeiting the bet.

By 10 p.m., I'm vibrating with need and Lee looks like he's barely holding on to his sanity. Finally, as the clock ticks over to 11 p.m., I reach for the bell on the counter to call last drinks—it is a Wednesday after all. But Lee beats me to it. He rings that bell like he's calling for help.

"Pay up," he bellows. "And get the *fuck* out!"

The locals ignore him, taking their sweet time. When the last customer leaves at 11:23, I flip the sign to CLOSED with hands that aren't quite steady.

"Mercy has already left," I say, not turning around. "Said she'd come in early to clean up after tonight."

"Smart woman."

I can hear him moving behind me, his footsteps deliberate and measured. When I finally turn, he's standing in the middle of the bar, hands loose at his sides, watching me with an intensity that steals my breath.

"Thirty-seven minutes," he says.

"Thirty-six," I correct, glancing at the clock.

"You want to wait?"

The question hangs between us, loaded with possibility. We could wait. We could honor our bet, sit on opposite sides of the bar and count down the final minutes like civilized people.

Or...

"No," I whisper. "I don't want to wait any longer."

Something snaps in his expression. In three long strides, he's across the room, his hands cupping my face as his mouth crashes down on mine. The kiss is desperate, hungry, two weeks of pent-up desire exploding between us like a dam bursting.

I melt into him, my hands fisting in his shirt as I kiss him back with everything I have. This is what I've been craving, what I've been dreaming about—his hands on me, his mouth claiming mine, the solid heat of his body pressed against every soft curve of mine.

"Fuck the bet," he growls against my lips. "I need you. Right now."

"Yes," I breathe. "God, yes."

He lifts me easily, setting me on the bar as his hands work at the buttons of my shirt. I reach for his belt, but he catches my wrists.

"Not fucking yet," he says, his voice rough with control. "I've been waiting for two weeks to get you completely naked. Don't you fucking dare deny me this."

"Lee—"

"Trust me."

I do. Completely and without question.

Every brush of his fingertips leaves goosebumps in their wake. When I'm finally naked, perched on the edge of the bar in nothing but a flush and the shimmer of neon light, he steps back.

His gaze drags over me slowly. Possessively. Like he's trying to decide where to start the feast.

"Jesus *fucking* Christ," he says, voice hoarse. "Look at you."

Then he's on me—mouth at my throat, lips parting over my skin, tongue dragging slow and wet across my collarbone before trailing lower. He palms my breast, squeezing just enough to make me gasp, then sucks my nipple into his mouth with a low groan.

My head tips back as he sucks harder, teeth grazing the tender peak, tongue swirling in maddening circles. He switches sides, pinching one nipple while he lavishes the other with his mouth, and I cry out.

"That's it," he murmurs, heat laced through every syllable. "Make those fucking sounds. I want this burned into your memory."

He kisses a line down my torso, stopping to flick his tongue into my belly button. My thighs shift open, desperate, slick. I can't stop moving, my hips rocking, aching to feel him anywhere.

He kneels, hands curling under my thighs and pulling me to the edge of the bar until I'm spread wide, open, throbbing.

"Look at this pussy," he groans, running his thumbs through my slick folds. "So wet. So perfect. You want my mouth, baby?"

"Yes—*please*, Lee."

He dives in without mercy.

His tongue licks a long, slow stripe up my center, from my entrance to my clit, and I jolt like I've been struck by lightning. He flattens his tongue and grinds into me, moaning as he drinks me in.

Then he zeroes in on my clit.

He circles it with obscene precision, gentle flicks followed by devastating suction, alternating pressure until I'm writhing, legs locked around his shoulders. Every time I start to come down, he switches it up, sucking, teasing, tracing patterns over the throbbing bundle of nerves until I'm on the edge again.

"Fuck, Lee, I—"

"Let go," he growls. "I want you to come on my tongue. Right now."

I break with a scream, orgasm ripping through me like wildfire. My thighs tremble, hips jerking, and he holds me down, his tongue relentless.

He shifts his grip, sliding one thick finger inside me, then another. He curls them perfectly, hitting that sweet, devastating spot.

"Lee, oh god—please—"

"You gonna come again?" he pants, mouth wet and glistening with my arousal. "Gonna soak my fingers this time?"

I nod frantically, clutching his hair like a lifeline.

"Then do it. Be a good girl and come all over me."

My second orgasm is even worse—white-hot and body-shaking, clenching around his fingers while he presses kisses to the inside of my thighs.

A phone alarm blares, cutting through my afterglow. I jerk, crunching up to stare down at him as he pulls it out, swiping to turn off the beeping.

"What's that?"

He stands slowly, licking his fingers.

Then he undoes his belt.

And holy. Shit.

His cock springs free—thick, flushed, gorgeous. It curves just slightly toward his belly, a prominent vein running up the shaft, the head shiny with precum. I lick my lips without thinking.

"That was midnight. Congratulations, Kya. You won."

His words register but I no longer care. His cock is far too distracting, and I am far too desperate to care. I want him in me. Now.

"I'm going to fuck you," he says, tone guttural. "So deep you'll feel me every time you move tomorrow."

He lines himself up, the head of his cock pressing hot and heavy against my entrance.

"You ready?" he asks. "You sure?"

"Please," I whisper. "I want to feel all of you."

He rolls a condom on then pushes in. I gasp as the stretch begins—my body yielding, molding around him inch by aching inch. It's too much and not enough, pressure building, nerves firing, pleasure and pain tangled into something deliciously unbearable.

"Jesus," he groans, jaw locked tight, sweat beading at his temples. "You're so fucking tight. I can feel your pussy gripping every inch of me."

My breath stutters, head falling back, and he doesn't stop until he's fully seated—hips flush with mine, the heavy weight of him pressing deep and perfect.

We stay there, locked together, panting. The fullness is dizzying. Intimate. Devastating.

"You feel like fucking heaven," he whispers, forehead pressed to mine. "Like you were made for me."

Then he pulls back—just a fraction—and slams in hard.

I scream.

Again.

Again.

His hips snap forward with a savage rhythm, each thrust hitting deeper, harder, sending wet, obscene sounds echoing through the room. The slap of skin against skin, our broken moans. It's raw, primal, feral.

He grabs my thigh, throws my leg over his shoulder, and the angle—fuck—it's everything. His cock hits that devastating spot inside me with ruthless precision.

"Oh god—Lee—right there—right there—"

"Yeah?" His voice is wrecked, breathless. "You like getting fucked on this bar like my personal fucktoy?"

"Yes," I gasp, wild. "Yes, I'm yours—I'm fucking yours—"

He drives in harder, deeper. "Say it again."

"I'm yours, Lee," I cry. "Yours. Yours. Yours."

He growls, grabs my jaw, and forces my gaze up to meet his. His eyes are wild, dark with possession and something deeper—reverence. Like he can't believe he gets to have me like this.

"Look at me when you come," he commands. "I want to watch you fall apart."

His thrusts become erratic, deeper and sharper, every stroke pushing me closer to the edge.

"I can't—Lee—please—"

"Yes, you fucking can." His thumb finds my clit and circles. "Come for me. Now."

And I shatter.

The orgasm tears through me like a tidal wave—full-body, toe-curling, so violent I scream. My muscles clamp around him, wet and pulsing, and he fucks me through every second of it like a man possessed.

My vision blurs. My ears ring. I'm wrecked, completely and utterly.

That's all it takes.

"Fuck—fuck, Kya—" Lee snarls, pulling out at the last second. He tears the condom off then pumps his cock once. Hot, thick ropes of cum spill across my belly and thighs as he curses, muscles tensed, back arched like a bowstring snapped taut.

We collapse into each other, chests heaving, bodies trembling. The air around us is hot and thick, heavy with sex and sweat and everything we didn't say but just proved with skin.

He presses a kiss to my temple, his hand still stroking up and down my side like he's grounding us both.

"You still with me?" he murmurs against my damp skin.

"Barely," I croak. My voice is raw, shredded. I don't even know if I'm still blinking evenly.

He chuckles, low and filthy and full of sin. "Good."

He leans up, eyes glittering.

"Because round two?" he says, brushing his fingers between my thighs, gathering the mess and slick still clinging to me. "That's going to be with your legs over my shoulders, your hands tied behind your back, and my cock buried so deep you'll *taste* me."

I shudder. "Please?"

Lee leans over me, eyes dark, lips parted. He looks wrecked, but not done. Not even close.

His gaze drops to the mess he's made on me. He drags his thumb through it, slow and reverent, smearing it across my skin.

"You look so fucking good like this," he murmurs, thumb tracing lazy circles over my hip. "You ready to head home for round two?"

I whimper, spent but still aching for more. I'm not sure I can make it without another round first.

Something in my gaze must have shown that 'cause he pauses. "You want more now?"

I nod.

"Then c'mere," he says roughly. He shifts back and gestures to the floor between his legs.

I know exactly what he wants.

And I want it too.

I slide down from the bar, knees hitting the cool wood. He's thick, glistening, already twitching with the promise of round two.

I lean forward and lick a slow stripe from the base to the tip of his cock.

He *hisses*, hips jerking.

"Fuck, Kya—"

"I'm just getting started," I whisper, wrapping my lips around the head and sucking him into my mouth.

His hand tangles in my hair instantly, grip firm but careful. I suck slow and deep, using my tongue to trace along the underside, teasing that sensitive spot just beneath the crown.

He groans, low, primal. His thighs flex under my hands as I bob my head, taking more each time, letting spit drip and coat him, making it messy and filthy and oh so satisfying.

"You're gonna make me come again if you keep that up," he grits out.

I pull off with a pop and look up at him through my lashes.

"That's kind of the point."

He lets out a strangled sound—half laugh, half fuck me—then grabs me under the arms and lifts me like I weigh nothing.

"Pool table," he growls. "Now."

He carries me across the room, both of us still slick and panting, and sets me on the cool felt top. I lie back, legs spreading as he steps between them.

But this time... there's no frantic edge.

He leans down, brushes our foreheads together. His hands cradle my face.

"You're incredible."

He kisses me, slow and deep and tender. Then he slides another condom on and presses against me.

The stretch makes me arch, makes me keen into his mouth. It's so much, so *full*, it blurs the line between pain and pleasure. He doesn't slam into me, he *sinks*, inch by thick, deliberate inch, until he's buried to the hilt, our bodies locked tight.

He stays there, letting me feel the heavy weight of him pulsing inside me, cock stretching me wide and filling every part of me. I feel it in my chest. My bones. My soul.

His hips roll into mine with a rhythm that feels designed to destroy me—long, dragging strokes that hit every sensitive nerve inside me. Every thrust is a grind, the thick head of his cock brushing my G-spot just right, the base dragging against my clit as he presses into me again and again.

The table creaks beneath us, the slick sound of him moving

inside me filling the air along with our ragged moans and whispered curses.

He threads his fingers through mine, pinning our joined hands beside my head.

"Eyes on me," he whispers, voice strained. "I want you right here with me."

I look at him. And I see it. Not just lust. Not just want.

Need. Raw, heart-wrecking, soul-deep need.

"I love you," I gasp, the words slipping out on a wave of emotion I can't stop or soften. "I love you."

He freezes, cock buried deep, his eyes wide and stunned. My heart stutters in my chest.

Then he cups my face, kisses me like he's starving for it, like the words unlocked something feral and fragile in him all at once.

"I love you too," he whispers against my lips. "So fucking much it scares me."

He starts to move again, harder, deeper, with purpose. But it's not just fucking now. Every thrust is a claim. Every roll of his hips is a vow. His cock glides in and out of me, thick and hot and devastating, dragging slick from my cunt with every retreat, making my whole body tremble.

He presses a hand between us, fingers finding my clit. He rubs slow, tight circles as he moves inside me, and the pressure builds fast. It's too much. Too perfect.

"I'm close," I choke. "I'm—oh god, Lee—"

"That's it," he pants. "Come for me. Come on my cock while I'm inside you."

I break.

My orgasm slams into me—white-hot, blinding. I scream his name as I clamp around him, pussy pulsing wildly, squeezing him so tight he growls, hips stuttering.

He follows me over the edge with a roar, burying himself deep and spilling inside me in thick, hot pulses.

He collapses onto me, and we stay like that for a long time, wrapped around each other, breathing hard and trying to process what just happened.

"Holy shit," I finally manage.

"Yeah," he agrees, pressing a soft kiss to my temple. "Holy shit."

"I won," I repeat, grinning.

"You won." He kisses me again, soft and sweet.

"Best bet I ever made," I agree.

He laughs. "I'll drink to that."

I close my eyes, savoring this moment. "Good thing Hawk's not installing those cameras until tomorrow."

"Is it? I wouldn't mind a replay."

Laughing, I kick him playfully with my foot.

"Ready to go home?"

As he helps me down from the bar and we gather our scattered clothes, I can't help but smile. He's right—coming back to Stoneheart, buying Devil's, falling in love with Lee Armstrong—it's all been the best gamble of my life.

XVA

18

KYA

The Saturday evening crowd at Devil's is steady but manageable. I'm behind the bar, trying not to watch the door every five minutes like some lovesick teenager.

Lee walks in just after seven, and my traitorous heart does a stupid skip. I smile but it slowly fades as I take him in. He looks tense, his jaw tight as he approaches the bar.

"Hey," I say, already reaching for his usual beer.

"Hey." He glances around, noting the crowd, then leans across the bar. "We need to talk. Can you take a break?"

My stomach drops. "Everything okay?"

"Yeah, just... come here for a sec?"

I follow him to the back office, anxiety building. He closes the door and immediately pulls me into his arms.

"I have to go out of town," he says against my hair. "Tonight. I've got to follow up on some Summit leads."

I pull back to look at him. "When will you be back?"

"Tomorrow night, late probably." His thumb strokes my cheek. "I'm sorry. I know tomorrow's your day off. I was planning to spend the whole day with you." The disappointment must show on my face because he kisses me softly. "I'll make it up to you."

"It's fine. This is important." I force a smile. "Besides, I should probably catch up on paperwork anyway."

A knock on the door interrupts us. Ginger pokes her head in, Tank visible behind her.

"Sorry to interrupt the goodbye kisses," she says, not looking sorry at all. "But Lee, the boys are ready to roll."

Lee sighs, pressing his forehead to mine. "I gotta go."

"Be safe," I whisper.

He kisses me once more, deep and promising, then heads out. Tank follows, but Ginger lingers, watching me.

"You look like someone just canceled Christmas," she observes.

"It's nothing. It's just that we had plans for tomorrow." I force a smile. "But it's fine. This is important."

"It is," she agrees, then her eyes light up dangerously. "Wait! This is perfect! Girls' night!"

"Ginger, I don't think—"

"No thinking! Just fun!" She pulls out her phone, already texting. "Tomorrow night, we're going out. And I mean *OUT* out. Not to some dive bar in Stoneheart where everyone knows us."

"I'm the only dive bar in Stoneheart," I point out dryly.

"Which is exactly why Steel's going to be our driver." She grins wickedly. "Poor boy owes me for making him help with Tank's surprise party planning. He'll drive us to Millbrook. We'll make a night of it."

Mercy appears from the stockroom. "Did I hear someone say girls' night?"

"Tomorrow," Ginger announces. "Millbrook. Dancing. Drinks. Debauchery."

"I'm in," Mercy says immediately. "God, I need to get laid. Or at least grind on someone who isn't wearing a wedding ring."

I look between them. "This is a terrible idea."

"The best ones always are," Ginger winks as she slides her phone back in her pocket. "Andi and Poppy are already confirmed. Steel will pick everyone up at seven."

"How did you—"

"I'm very efficient." She heads for the door. "Wear something slutty!"

I glance at Mercy. "You know this is a terrible idea, right?"

She laughs, slapping me on the shoulder. "Can't wait."

~

At 7pm on the dot, Steel parks a large SUV in my drive. He looks like he's heading to his own execution, while Ginger, who's in the passenger seat, is practically bouncing with excitement.

"Get in, losers! We're going shopping!" she yells out the window.

"That's not how the quote goes," Poppy says, sliding in and shuffling over. She's glowing in a flowy blue top that accommodates her small bump.

"Just get in," Ginger retorts.

Andi claims the back row with Mercy, who's wearing a black dress so short I'm concerned about her getting a misdemeanour for public indecency.

"Looking to catch someone tonight?" I tease.

"Looking to catch something," Mercy mutters. "It's been months. MONTHS! My vagina is growing cobwebs"

"TMI," Steel groans from the driver's seat.

"Oh honey," Ginger turns to him with a wicked grin. "It's only going to get worse. Now drive! Millbrook awaits!"

The hour-long drive is chaos. Ginger controls the playlist, cycling through everything from 90s hip-hop to current pop. Mercy keeps making increasingly inappropriate comments about what she wants to do to the first hot guy she sees, while Andi and Poppy share embarrassing stories about their men.

"Did I ever tell you about the time Hawk got stuck in the playground equipment?" Andi asks.

"No!" we all scream in unison.

"He was showing off for the twins, tried to go down the slide, and his shoulders got wedged. Steel had to cut him out."

"You didn't tell me!" Poppy yells at him.

He hunches his shoulders, staring stubbornly out the windscreen at the road.

"Please tell me there are photos," Ginger begs.

"Oh, there's video."

"I should have stayed home," Steel mutters as we shriek with laughter.

"And miss all this female bonding?" Ginger pats his arm. "Besides, Tank specifically volunteered you."

"Tank threw me under the bus," Steel corrects.

The Green Room is everything Devil's isn't. Neon lights pulse in time with the bass, the air thick with perfume and possibility. The crowd is young, dressed to impress, and blissfully unaware of who we are.

"First round's on me!" Ginger announces, dragging us to the bar. The bartender, a twenty-something with too much gel in his hair, openly stares at her cleavage.

"Eyes up here, junior," she says, snapping her fingers. "Five tequila shots and…" she glances at Steel, "one water for our designated driver."

The bartender slides our drinks across and we all reach for our glass.

"Good boy," she pinches Steel's cheek after he accepts the water.

"To girls' night!" Poppy raises her mocktail.

"To getting laid!" Mercy adds.

"To new friends!" Andi chimes in.

"To not overthinking everything!" I contribute.

"TO STEEL FOR DRIVING!" Ginger shouts.

We down the shots (except Steel and Poppy), and immediately hit the dance floor. The music is some remix I don't recognize, but it doesn't matter. Ginger grabs my hands, spinning me around while Andi, Mercy and Poppy follow, laughing.

"This is what you needed!" Ginger yells over the music. "To remember you're young and hot and alive!"

She's not wrong. For the first time in weeks, I'm not thinking about the bar, or bills, or Summit. I'm just dancing with my friends, letting the music move through me.

Mercy disappears for a song, returning with her lipstick smudged.

"Already?" Andi asks, impressed.

"What can I say? When you know, you know." She grins. "He's got a friend if you know anyone who might be interested."

"Pass," I laugh. "I'm taken."

"Disgustingly taken," Ginger agrees. "She and Lee are nauseating."

"Says the woman who made us all watch while Tank fed her strawberries at her birthday," Poppy points out.

"It was romantic!"

"It was soft-core porn!"

When we tire of dancing, Ginger drags us down the street to a second stop. This one is quieter, more upscale. Exposed brick walls, Edison bulbs, and bartenders in suspenders.

"I need food," Poppy declares as we claim a corner booth.

"Nachos!" Ginger points at the menu. "Steel, order us nachos! And those little slider things. And mozzarella sticks!"

"Why do I have to—"

"Because you're sober and we love you," she says, patting his head like a puppy.

Steel sighs. "How is this my life?"

"You joined an MC," I remind him, more than a little tipsy. "Isn't this is what you signed up for?"

"No one mentioned I'd be babysitting for drunk women."

"We're not drunk!" Ginger protests, then immediately knocks over her water glass. "That was the table's fault."

While Steel orders, Mercy regales us with stories from her bartending days before Devil's.

"There was this guy who came in every Thursday, ordered milk. MILK. In a bar!"

"Maybe he had ulcers," Poppy suggests.

"Maybe he was a serial killer," Andi counters.

"He was definitely a serial killer," Ginger agrees. "Steel, are you writing this down? This is important information we should pass on to Lee for Kya's safety."

"I'm not your secretary," Steel says, but he's fighting a smile.

The food arrives and we attack it like we haven't eaten in days. Ginger steals everyone's pickles, Andi and Poppy share the mozzarella sticks, and Mercy keeps checking her phone.

"Supply closet guy?" I ask.

"His name is Derek. He wants to meet up again later."

"Derek!" Ginger shouts, causing the entire bar to turn. "Absolutely not! I'm not letting you sleep with a man called Derek!"

"Inside voice," Steel pleads.

"I don't have an inside voice! I have a Ginger voice and a LOUDER GINGER VOICE!"

An older woman at the next table leans over. "You girls having a bachelorette party?"

"No," Ginger says seriously. "We're having a 'Lee's out of town and Kya needs to remember she's a bad bitch' party."

The woman laughs. "In that case, next round's on me."

Somehow she and her friends end up in our gang for the night as we drag Steel from one place to another.

The clubs begin to blur together until I'm lost in the chaos. Wherever we are has three floors with different music on each level, and more people than the entire population of Stoneheart.

"I love this place!" Ginger screams, dragging us to the middle floor where they're playing early 2000s hits.

Poor Steel has positioned himself by the wall, looking like a bodyguard. Several women have tried to approach him, but he just points to us and shakes his head.

"You know what your problem is?" Ginger says, slinging an arm around me as we take a break from dancing.

"I have a problem?"

"You think too much." She cups my face, her eyes serious despite the glitter someone threw that's now stuck to her cheeks. "Lee loves you. You love him. Stop worrying about all the what-ifs and just BE HAPPY."

"Ginger, it's not like that. We already—"

"It is EXACTLY like that." She spins me around to face the dance floor. "Look at Andi. She overthought everything with Hawk and almost lost him. Now look at her!"

Andi is indeed dancing like no one's watching, laughing as Poppy attempts to twerk with her baby belly.

"That boy would burn down the world for you," Ginger continues. "And you'd do the same for him."

"How do you know?"

"Because you get the same look Tank gets when someone threatens me." She smiles, softer now. "Like you'd kill anyone who hurt him."

"I already told him I love him, and he said the same."

She blinks then laughs. "So my speech was unnecessary?"

"Yes." Impulsively, I hug her. "But thank you anyway."

We stay until the lights come on at 2 AM, Ginger somehow convincing the DJ to play "Closing Time" as we gather our things.

"I need nuggets," Mercy announces as we stumble drunkenly down the sidewalk to Steel's SUV.

"Nuggets!" Ginger agrees. "Steel, we need nuggets!"

"There's food at home—"

"NUGGETS, STEEL."

The poor drive-through worker looks overwhelmed as four drunk women and one pregnant one shout orders from the car.

"Twenty nuggets!"

"No, forty!"

"And fries!"

"Large fries!"

"Apple pies!"

"Do they still have those?"

"STEEL, ASK IF THEY HAVE APPLE PIES!"

Steel turns to the speaker with a defeated expression. "Can I get sixty nuggets, five large fries, and however many apple pies you have? Add six bottles of water to that as well."

"I got it!" Ginger waves her credit card. "Tank gave me his card!"

"That's Tank's?" I ask.

"He'll never notice. I bought a motorcycle last month and he didn't say anything."

"You bought a—"

"NUGGETS ARE READY!" Steel shouts tossing takeout bags into the back of the vehicle like we're wild animals.

To be fair to him, we act like it as we rip the bags open, shoving food into our mouths like we haven't been fed in five years.

We're all significantly quieter now, full of nuggets and exhausted from dancing. Mercy's the first to pass out against the window. Poppy's dozing, humming something off-key as she closes her eyes, a hand over her belly. Meanwhile, Andi's braiding Ginger's hair.

"Steel," Ginger says seriously, nugget crumbs on her dress. "You're a good prospect."

"Thanks?"

"I mean it. You took care of us tonight. You didn't complain. Well, not much. That's what family does."

He glances at her in the rearview mirror. "You ladies aren't so bad."

"We're amazing," she corrects.

As we drive through the night, I can't help but smile. These women, this strange found family–it's more than I ever expected when I came back to Stoneheart.

"Hey Kya," Ginger says sleepily. "Lee's probably already home."

My pulse quickens. "You think?"

"I know. Tank texted. They got back an hour ago."

We stop at Andi's first, Hawk coming out to carry her inside. Then Poppy's, where Axel is waiting on the porch. Mercy gets dropped at her apartment. Steel half-carries her inside as she yells at us how much she can't wait until the next one.

Finally, it's just me, Ginger, and Steel.

"I'm putting in a good word with Stone about you," Ginger tells Steel as we pull up to her and Tank's house.

"Thanks, Ginger."

She leans over and kisses his cheek, leaving a red lipstick mark. "You're gonna be a great brother someday soon."

Tank appears, scooping his drunk wife into his arms. "Have fun, baby?"

"The best! Steel was amazing! Can we keep him?"

"He's not a puppy," Tank laughs, nodding at Steel. "Thanks for keeping them safe."

By the time Steel pulls up to my cottage, I'm mostly sober, the cool night air having cleared my head during the drive.

"Thanks, Steel. For everything tonight."

He gives me a rare full smile. "Lee's bike is here."

I look, and sure enough, there it is parked by my door.

"Get some sleep, Steel."

I exit the vehicle as Lee opens my door. He leans against it, arms crossed, one leg folded over the other as he smirks at me.

I wanna ride that man like a stripper pole.

"Yes ma'am," Steel says. "And Kya?"

I glance back at him.

"Have fun."

He drives off with a knowing smirk, leaving me standing in my driveway, heart racing with anticipation. The night is quiet except for the distant sound of Steel's car fading away.

I watch Lee watching me, a shiver of desire snaking down my back.

Time to rock his world.

19

KYA

Lee pushes off from my doorframe as I approach, uncrossing his arms with that lazy confidence that makes heat pool low in my belly. The porch light casts shadows across his face, highlighting the sharp line of his jaw, the fullness of his lips.

"Have fun?" he asks, voice low and rough.

"The best." I sway slightly on my heels, the tequila making me brave and reckless. "Steel was our designated driver. We made him stop for nuggets."

"Nuggets?" He's fighting a smile, and I want to kiss it off his face.

"Sixty of them." I step closer, close enough to smell his cologne mixed with leather and the night air. "But I'm done talking about nuggets."

His eyes darken as I reach out, running one finger down the center of his chest, feeling his muscles tense under my touch.

"Kya—"

"All night," I interrupt, circling him slowly, my fingers trailing across his shoulders. "All night I danced with my girls. Had men offering to buy me drinks, trying to get my number." I stop behind him, going up on my tiptoes to whisper in his ear. "And all I could think about was you."

He turns to face me, but I dance back, keeping just out of reach.

"Thought about your hands," I continue, backing toward my front door, holding his gaze. "Your mouth. The way you look at me like you want to devour me."

"Kya." My name comes out strained.

"Are you going to devour me, Lee?" I reach behind me for the door handle, missing it twice before finding it. "Or are you going to stand there all night?"

The door swings open and I stumble backward, laughing when he catches me around the waist. His hands are large and warm through the thin fabric of my dress, fingers spanning nearly my entire waist.

"Careful," he murmurs, but I'm already pulling him inside, kicking the door shut with my heel.

"I don't want to be careful." I press against him, feeling every hard line of his body. "I want to be wild. Reckless." I nip at his jaw, tasting the salt of his skin. "I want to make you lose control."

His hands tighten on my waist. "You're drunk."

"Tipsy," I correct, sliding my hands under his shirt, feeling his abs contract under my touch. "And I know exactly what I want."

"What do you want?"

Instead of answering, I drop to my knees.

"Fuck, Kya—"

I look up at him through my lashes as my hands work at his belt, taking my time with the buckle. "I thought about this during girls' night. When Mercy was talking about supply closet Derek and what she wanted to do to him."

His hands fist at his sides. "Who the fuck is Derek?"

"Nobody." I get his belt undone, moving to the button of his jeans. "Just some random guy who doesn't matter. Not like you."

I lower his zipper tooth by tooth, watching his chest rise and fall with increasingly ragged breaths. When I hook my fingers in his waistband, he stops me.

"Bedroom," he growls, hauling me to my feet.

"Here is good—"

He silences me with a kiss that steals my breath, his tongue claiming mine with a thoroughness that makes my knees weak. When we break apart, I'm panting.

"Bedroom," he repeats, and this time I don't argue.

He walks me backward down the hall, his hands roaming my body, finding the zipper of my dress and drawing it down slowly. The dress pools at my feet just as we reach the bedroom, leaving me in a black lace set.

"Christ," he breathes, taking me in. The bra is all delicate lace and strategic cutouts, the panties barely there. "You wore this to the club?"

"Under my dress." I do a slow turn, letting him see how the panties are essentially just string in the back. "It made me feel powerful."

"Did it just."

"Yes." I face him again, stepping closer. "But you know what makes me feel more powerful?"

"What?"

"The way you're looking at me right now. Like you can't decide whether to worship me or ruin me."

"Both," he says roughly. "Definitely both."

I reach for his shirt, unbuttoning it with fingers that tremble slightly from want rather than alcohol. Each button reveals more skin—his chest with its light dusting of hair, the V of his hips, the trail that disappears beneath his jeans.

"My turn to look," I murmur, pushing the shirt off his shoulders.

The moonlight from the window highlights every muscle, every scar, every inch of him that I've memorized but never get tired of exploring. I run my hands over his chest, feeling his heart race under my palm.

"You're so beautiful," I whisper, then laugh at myself. "Is it weird to call a man beautiful?"

"From you? No." He cups my face gently. "Nothing from you is weird."

The tenderness in his voice makes my chest tight. I kiss him again, slower this time, savoring the slide of his tongue against mine, the way he groans when I suck on his bottom lip.

"I need you," I whisper against his mouth.

"You have me."

"No, I mean—" I push his jeans down, frustrated with the barriers between us. "I need you now."

He kicks off his jeans and boxers, then lifts me easily, carrying me to the bed. But instead of following me down, he stands at the edge, just looking.

"What?" I ask, suddenly self-conscious.

"Just memorizing this." His hands slide up my legs, from my ankles to my thighs, slowly, reverently. "You in that lingerie. Your hair all wild. That flush on your skin."

"Less memorizing, more touching."

He chuckles, but complies, his hands continuing their journey up my body. When he reaches the edge of my panties, he hooks his fingers in them, dragging them down torturously slowly.

"Lee," I whine, lifting my hips.

"Patience."

"I left my patience at the club."

He tosses my panties aside, then spreads my legs wider, settling between them. But instead of touching me where I need him, he kisses the inside of my knee.

"I'm going to take my time with you," he says against my skin, moving higher with each kiss. "Going to taste every inch of you."

"Please—"

"Gonna to make you beg," he continues, his breath hot against my inner thigh. "Make you shake. Make you scream."

"Big talk," I manage, though my voice comes out breathless.

He looks up at me, eyes dark with promise. "Want me to prove it?"

"God, yes."

His mouth is on me then, and I cry out, my back arching off the bed. He wasn't lying about taking his time—he explores me like he's got all night, alternating between soft kisses and firm strokes of his tongue, building me up only to back off just before I break.

"Lee, please," I beg, my hands fisted in his hair.

"Please what?"

"I need—I need—"

"Tell me."

"I need to come. Please, I need—"

He sucks on my clit while sliding two fingers inside me, curling them just right, and I shatter. The orgasm rolls through me in waves, each one more intense than the last, until I'm trembling and gasping his name.

He kisses his way up my body, giving me time to recover. When he reaches my bra, he makes quick work of the clasp, tossing it aside.

"Beautiful," he murmurs, taking one nipple into his mouth.

I arch into him, still sensitive from my orgasm, every touch feeling like electricity. When I can form coherent thoughts again, I push at his shoulders, rolling us so I'm on top.

"My turn," I say, straddling his hips.

His hands go to my waist, but I pin them to the bed. "No touching. Not yet."

"Kya—"

"I told you I wanted to be wild tonight." I roll my hips, feeling him hard against me but not taking him inside yet. "This is me being wild."

I torture us both, sliding against him, getting him wet with my arousal but never quite taking him in. His hands clench in the sheets, his jaw tight with the effort of control.

"Kya, baby, please—"

"Now who's begging?"

"Me," he says without hesitation. "I'm begging. Now fuck me or I'll take over."

I reach for the nightstand, grabbing protection and rolling it on him slowly, maintaining eye contact the whole time. Then, finally, I sink down onto him.

We both groan at the sensation. I'm still sensitive and swollen, and he feels bigger than usual, stretching me perfectly.

"Fuck," he breathes. "You feel incredible."

I start to move, finding a rhythm that has us both gasping. His hands are on my hips now, helping me ride him, and I don't stop him this time. I need his touch, need his strength, need him.

"Look at you," he says, voice rough with awe. "So fucking beautiful like this. Taking what you want."

"You," I gasp. "I want you."

"You have me. All of me."

The way he says it, the raw honesty in his voice, breaks me open. I slow my movements, leaning down to kiss him deeply.

"I love you," I whisper against his lips.

He rolls us, never breaking our connection, until he's above me. "I love you too, Kya."

The wildness from before shifts into something deeper, more intense. We move together slowly now, savoring each touch, each kiss, each whispered word of love. When he slides his hand between us to touch me, I'm already so close.

"Together," I plead. "I want to come together."

"Yeah, baby. Together."

We find our release at the same time, holding each other through the waves of pleasure.

After, he pulls me against his chest, and I can feel his heart racing under my palm, matching the rhythm of mine.

"Wild enough for you?" I ask, my voice rough.

He laughs, pressing a kiss to my hair. "Perfect. You're perfect."

"Even when I'm tipsy and demanding?"

"Especially then." His arms tighten around me. "Though I have to ask—who the fuck is supply closet Derek?"

I giggle, the sound slightly hysterical from exhaustion and satisfaction. "Some guy Mercy tried to hook up with at the club."

"And that made you think of me?"

"No." I tilt my head to look at him. "It made me think how glad I am that I get to come home to this. To you. To us."

His expression softens. "Yeah?"

"I'm the luckiest woman alive," I tell him, meaning every word despite the alcohol still in my system. "I get to love you. I get to be loved by you."

"Kya—"

"I mean it." I cup his face, making sure he can see my sincerity. "Tonight was fun. The girls are amazing. But nothing compares to coming home to you."

He kisses me softly, tenderly, like I'm something precious.

The simple gesture makes my eyes sting with unexpected tears. "I don't deserve you."

"Other way around, baby." He pulls the covers over us, tucking me against his side. "Sleep now. You're going to have a hell of a hangover tomorrow."

"I don't get hangovers," I mumble, already drifting. "I'm lucky like that."

"Yeah?"

"Mmm. Got to be wild. Got to come home to you. No hang over. Perfect night."

His chest rumbles with quiet laughter. "Love you, my wild girl."

"Love you too," I whisper, and fall asleep feeling cherished, satisfied, and completely, utterly home.

20

KYA

Three weeks later

The Stoneheart MC clubhouse is alive with music, laughter, and the kind of easy camaraderie that comes from family celebrating together. Someone's got a guitar out, Cash is holding court at the bar with Mercy. The smell of barbecue drifts in from the back patio where Hawk is manning the grill, while around us kids run through the house, screaming with laughter.

I'm curled up on one of the worn leather couches, Lee's arm around me, watching it all with a sense of wonder that still catches me off guard. Three months ago, I wasn't sure I wanted to return to Stoneheart. Now I'm home .

"I called Emma this morning," Lee says quietly, his fingers tracing patterns on my shoulder.

My heart skips. "You did? What did you tell her?"

"That you're back in town and we're together. She screamed so loud I think she damaged my eardrum."

"Good screaming or bad screaming?"

"The kind of screaming that comes with 'I fucking knew it!' and 'about damn time!'" He chuckles. "She's planning to come home for Christmas."

The words make my chest tight with emotion.

"I look forward to it."

I used to watch Lee from across the room, certain he was untouchable, unreachable. Emma's gorgeous older brother who could never be mine. And now here I am. Once the girl everyone whispered about, Patty Sullivan's daughter with no future and fewer options. Now I have Lee's name on my back, a family that chose me, a business that's thriving, and a town that's backed me when it mattered most.

The transformation feels surreal, like I'm living someone else's life.

I gesture around the room. "Six months ago, if someone had told me I'd be here, at an MC party, blissfully happy... I'd have laughed."

"And now?"

I look up at him, this man who's become my anchor, my safe harbor, my everything. "Now I can't imagine being anywhere else."

His smile is soft, private, the one he saves just for me. "Good. Because you're stuck with us now."

"Poor me," I tease, then squeal as he tickles my ribs in retaliation.

"Hey, lovebirds," Bones calls out from across the room. "Save the foreplay for later. We're trying to have a civilized party here."

"This is civilized?" Mercy asks, gesturing to where two prospects are engaged in what appears to be an arm-wrestling tournament that's devolved into a full wrestling match on the floor.

"For us? Yeah," Cash says with a grin. "You should see what our unruly parties look like."

"I'm not sure I want to," I reply, though I'm smiling. This is everything I never knew I needed.

Stone approaches our couch, a beer in each hand. He hands me one.

"Welcome to the family, kid."

I gulp, fighting back tears. "Thanks."

Lee's arm tightens around me. "Hey," he says softly. "You okay?"

"Yeah." I laugh at myself. "Sorry. It's just... I've never really had this before."

"Well, you do now," Duck says, appearing beside Stone with his wife on his arm. "And we don't let go easy."

Maggie, a petite woman with kind eyes and silver-streaked hair, reaches out to squeeze my hand. "I hope you know how happy we all are that you're here. Lee's been like a different person since you came back to town."

"Different how?" I ask, curious.

"Settled," she says simply. "Happy. It seems he's finally found what he was looking for."

I glance at Lee, who's gone slightly pink around the ears. "Is that so?"

"Ginger's got a big mouth," he mutters, but there's affection in his voice.

"Maggie's right," Stone adds. "You're good for him, Kya. Good for all of us. Devil's has become the heart of this community again because of what you've done there."

"I just cleaned it up and fixed the beer taps," I protest.

"I believe *I* fixed the taps," Lee says, earning himself an elbow in the ribs.

"You did more than that," Bones says, joining our little circle. "You made it a place people want to be again."

There's a sharp rap on the clubhouse door. One of the prospects disengages from the wrestling session and returns a minute later, Josie Bright trailing him.

"My apologies for the interruption," she says, glancing around. "But I have some good news." She hands Stone a folder. "The council voted down the first residential rezoning bill. As of this morning, the proposal is dead in the water."

A cheer goes up from the brothers who've gathered around to listen. Lee's hand finds mine, squeezing tight.

"What changed their minds?" I ask.

Her sharp gaze turns to me. "It seems your victory at Devil's was a strong motivator. When they couldn't intimidate you into selling, it sent a message to the rest of the property owners in the area. My office has been inundated with parties interested in being represented."

"So it's over?"

"This phase of it, yes. They'll be back eventually—companies like Summit always are. But you bought the community time, and you proved they can be beaten. Legally." She says the last word as she glares at Stone. He meets her gaze with his own.

The cheer that goes up this time is deafening. Someone cranks up the music, drinks flow freely, and the party kicks into high gear. I'm passed from person to person, receiving congratulations, hearing stories, and getting pulled into the kind of easy banter that makes my heart full.

It's nearly midnight when Lee finally rescues me from a heated discussion with Cash about the best way to make nachos.

"Dance with me," he says, pulling me toward the small clearing that's serving as a makeshift dance floor.

"You don't dance," I point out, though I follow him willingly.

"Sure I do." He pulls me into his arms just as the current song ends and something slow and sweet starts playing. "Perfect timing."

We sway together in the dim light, and I close my eyes, letting myself sink into the moment. His hands are warm and sure on my back, his heartbeat steady against my cheek. Around us, the party continues, but it feels like we're in our own little bubble.

"Thank you," I whisper.

"For what?"

"For this. For them. For giving me somewhere I belong."

"This is your home, Kya."

"I know. I can feel it." I pull back to look at him. "I love you."

"I love you too." He leans down to kiss me, soft and sweet. "Ready to get out of here?"

"God, yes."

We say our goodbyes, which takes another twenty minutes because apparently leaving an MC party requires hugging everyone individually and promising to attend the next one. By the time we make it to Lee's bike, I'm exhausted but happy, my heart full to bursting.

The ride to my cottage is peaceful, the night air cool against my skin. When we pull into my driveway, I'm already thinking about getting Lee naked and expressing my gratitude for this perfect evening in the most thorough way possible.

"What are you thinking about?" he asks as we walk up the path to my front door.

"You. Naked. In my bed. Immediately."

He stops walking so abruptly I nearly run into him. "Jesus, Kya."

"What? It's been a perfect night, and I want to end it properly." I unlock the front door and turn to face him. "Unless you're too tired?"

His laugh is low and rough. "Never too tired for you."

The moment we're inside, he's on me. His hands are in my hair, his mouth claiming mine with a hunger that sets my blood on fire. I kiss him back just as desperately, my hands working at his cut, needing to feel skin.

"Bedroom," I gasp between kisses.

"Too far," he growls, backing me against the front door.

His hands are everywhere—skimming up my thighs, bunching my dress around my waist, finding the edge of my panties and stroking over the damp fabric.

"Lee—"

"Right here," he says, dropping to his knees. "Can't wait."

He hooks his fingers in the waistband of my underwear and drags them down my legs. Then his mouth is on me, and I have to bite my lip to keep from crying out loud enough to wake the neighbors.

He knows exactly how to touch me now, exactly what I need. Within minutes, I'm shaking apart against his mouth, my hands fisted in his hair as waves of pleasure crash over me.

"Bedroom," he says when I finally come back to myself. "Now."

This time I don't argue. I take his hand and lead him down the hall, both of us shedding clothes as we go. By the time we reach my bed, we're both naked and desperate.

Lee lifts me onto the mattress, following me down and covering my body with his. The weight of him, the heat, the feeling of being completely surrounded by him—it's everything I need.

"I love you," he whispers as he enters me, slow and deep.

"I love you too," I whisper back.

We move together in perfect synchronization, building toward something that's more than just physical release. This is connection, communion, the deepest expression of what we mean to each other.

When I come, it's with his name on my lips and my eyes locked on his. He follows me over the edge, burying his face in my neck as he empties himself inside me.

Afterward, we lie tangled together, breathing hard and utterly spent.

"That was..." I start.

"Perfect," he finishes.

"I was going to say earth-shattering, but perfect works."

He chuckles, pressing a kiss to my temple. "Tonight was perfect. All of it."

"Even the part where Bones nearly dropped me during that hug?"

"Especially that part. Gave me an excuse to be possessive."

I laugh, turning in his arms so I can see his face. "You don't need an excuse for that."

"Good to know." His expression grows serious. "Are you happy, Kya? Really happy?"

"Happier than I've ever been in my life," I tell him honestly. "I have you, I have the bar, I have a family. What more could I want?"

"A ring on your finger?"

I sit up, staring down at him. "Are you serious?"

"Deadly." He sits up as well, taking my hands in his. "I love you, Kya Sullivan. I love your stubborn streak and your smart mouth and the way you take care of everyone around you. I love that you came back to this town and made it better just by being here. I don't want to wait for someday. Marry me."

Tears blur my vision as I stare at this man who's become my everything. "Lee..."

"I know it's fast," he says quickly. "I know we've only been together a few months. But I've never been more sure of anything in my life. You're it for me, Kya. You're my home, my family, my future. Say yes."

"Yes," I say, throwing my arms around his neck. "I love you so much."

"I love you too, future Mrs. Armstrong."

"Future Mrs. Armstrong," I repeat, testing how it sounds. "I like it."

"Good," he says, pulling me down for a kiss. "Because you're stuck with me now. Forever."

"Promise?"

"Promise."

We fall asleep wrapped around each other. I dream of a future filled with motorcycle rides and bar crowds and the kind of love that lasts forever. When I wake up, Lee is still there, still mine, and there's a ring on my finger that's proof this isn't a dream.

I'm home. And I'm never leaving again.

EPILOGUE
KYA

Five Months Later

The waiting room at Stoneheart General Hospital buzzes with nervous energy and the kind of barely contained chaos that follows the Stoneheart MC wherever they go. I'm curled up in one of the uncomfortable plastic chairs, Lee's leather cut draped over my shoulders, watching the controlled mayhem unfold around me.

Bones is pacing a hole in the linoleum floor, muttering under his breath about how long labor is supposed to take. Duck sits stoically in the corner, his wife Maggie knitting something tiny and yellow. Hawk stands by the windows like a sentinel, periodically checking his phone for updates from Axel.

"Any word?" Lee asks, returning from the vending machine with two cups of coffee that smell like they were brewed sometime last week.

"Nothing yet." I accept the coffee gratefully, even though it tastes like sludge. "Hawk says it could be hours still."

"First babies take their time," Maggie agrees without looking up from her knitting. "Poppy's young and strong. Everything will be fine."

I hope she's right. Poppy and Axel have been through hell to get to this point. They deserve this happiness.

The elevator dings, and I look up to see Mercy and Cash stepping out together. They're trying to look casual, but there's something in their body language—the careful distance between them—that makes me bite back a smile.

"Any news?" Mercy asks, settling into the chair beside me.

"Still waiting," I reply, then lower my voice. "Interesting entrance you two made."

Mercy's cheeks go pink. "We just happened to arrive at the same time."

"Uh-huh." I glance at Cash, who's suddenly very interested in the outdated magazines on the side table. "And I suppose that hickey on your neck is from running into a door?"

Her hand flies to her throat. "Kya!"

"I'm just saying, if you two are going to sneak around, you might want to invest in some concealer."

Before Mercy can respond, the elevator opens again and Stone steps out, followed by Josie Bright. The lawyer looks impeccable as always—not a hair out of place, her suit perfectly pressed—but there's something different about her tonight. A softness around the edges that wasn't there before.

Stone, on the other hand, looks like he's been running his hands through his hair. His usually perfect appearance is slightly rumpled, and there's an energy about him that's distinctly un-presidential.

"Jesus," Lee mutters under his breath. "Everyone's getting laid but us."

I elbow him in the ribs. "We got laid three hours ago."

"That was three hours ago. I have needs."

"You have a problem."

"A problem that you created by being irresistible."

Despite everything—the hospital setting, the worry about Poppy, the exhaustion from being here all night—I feel that familiar flutter of heat low in my belly.

"Down, boy," I murmur. "This is neither the time nor the place."

"There's always time," he says, but he's grinning as he says it. "And I can find a place."

Stone approaches our little group, and I notice the way his eyes track to Josie as she settles into a chair across the room. She's pulled out her phone and appears to be working, but I catch her glancing his way more than once.

"How's Axel holding up?" Stone asks.

"About as well as you'd expect," Lee replies. "Hawk had to physically restrain him from threatening a doctor an hour ago."

"Can't blame him. Waiting's the hardest part."

Across the room, Josie looks up from her phone, and for just a moment, her gaze meets Stone's. The air between them practically crackles with tension before she looks away, color staining her cheeks.

Oh, this is interesting.

"Josie," I call out. "Come sit with us. No point in sitting alone."

She hesitates, glancing at Stone, then makes her way over. "Thanks. Hospitals aren't exactly my favorite place."

"Nobody's favorite place," Stone says, and there's something gentle in his tone that makes me look at him more closely.

"True." Josie settles into the chair next to mine, and I catch a whiff of her perfume—something expensive and sophisticated. "How long have you all been here?"

"Since about ten last night," Bones answers, finally stopping his pacing long enough to join the conversation. "Axel called when Poppy's water broke, and here we are."

"It's sweet," Josie says. "The way you all show up for each other."

"That's what family does," Duck says from his corner. "Show up."

Something flickers across Josie's face—longing, maybe, or wistfulness. I wonder about her story, about what brought her to Stoneheart and whether she has family of her own somewhere.

Hawk's phone buzzes loudly. He answers it immediately, his expression intense as he listens.

"Yeah... okay... we'll be right there."

He hangs up, and the entire waiting room goes silent.

"Well?" Bones demands.

Hawk's typically stoic expression cracks into a rare smile. "It's a girl. Eight pounds, two ounces. Both mom and baby are healthy."

The cheer that goes up is loud enough to wake half the hospital. Maggie starts crying happy tears, Duck actually cracks a smile, and Bones looks like he might pass out from relief.

"Can we see them?" Mercy asks.

"Give them a few minutes to get settled, then family can go in. Two at a time."

"I should go," Josie says, standing. "This is family time."

"You're family," Stone says firmly, catching her wrist as she moves to leave. "Stay."

The touch is brief—just his fingers around her wrist—but the effect is immediate. Josie goes completely still, her breath catching audibly. When Stone realizes what he's done, he releases her quickly, but the damage is done. Whatever careful distance they've been maintaining just evaporated.

"I—" Josie starts.

"Please. Stay."

She nods mutely and sits back down, but I notice she chooses a different chair—one that's not quite so close to Stone.

The next hour passes in a blur of excitement. Axel emerges looking shell-shocked and blissful, showing off pictures on his phone of the tiniest, most perfect baby I've ever seen. When it's finally Lee's and my turn to meet the newest member of the Stoneheart family, I'm not prepared for the emotional sucker punch that hits me.

Poppy looks radiant despite her exhaustion, cradling a bundle of pink blankets like she's holding the most precious thing in the world. Because she is.

"Meet Rose," she says softly, angling the baby so we can see her face.

She's perfect. Absolutely, completely perfect, with a tiny button nose and the softest wisps of dark hair. When she opens her eyes, they're the same piercing blue as her father's.

"She's beautiful," I whisper, afraid to speak too loudly and disturb her.

"Want to hold her?" Poppy asks.

My heart stops. "I—are you sure?"

"Of course."

With infinite care, I take the baby from her mother's arms. Rose is so small, so delicate, but she settles against me like she belongs there. When she wraps her tiny fingers around mine, something shifts inside my chest, a longing so sharp and unexpected it takes my breath away.

"Hey there, little one," I murmur. "Welcome to the world."

I look up to find Lee watching me with an expression I can't quite read. There's tenderness there, and something else, something that makes my pulse quicken.

"Natural," he says softly.

"What?"

"You. With her. You're a natural."

Heat floods my cheeks as I realize what he's implying. We've never talked about kids—not seriously. But looking down at this perfect little person, feeling the weight of her in my arms, I can suddenly picture it. A little boy with Lee's green eyes. A little girl with his stubborn streak and my determination.

"Lee—"

"I know. Not yet." He steps closer, pressing a kiss to my temple. "But someday?"

"Someday," I agree, my voice barely a whisper.

When we finally emerge from the room, the waiting area has cleared out considerably. Most of the brothers have headed home, leaving just the core group—Stone, Duck and Maggie, Mercy and Cash, and Josie.

"How are they?" Maggie asks immediately.

"Perfect," I say, and mean it. "Absolutely perfect."

"Good." She beams. "I'll bring food by tomorrow. New parents need to eat."

"I should head home too," Josie says, gathering her purse. "Early court date tomorrow."

"I'll walk you to your car," Stone offers, so casually it would sound polite if not for the way his voice drops slightly on the words.

"That's not necessary—"

"It's three in the morning. It's necessary."

Josie looks like she wants to argue, but something in Stone's expression stops her. "Fine. Thank you."

As they head toward the elevator, I catch the way Stone's hand hovers protectively at her back, the way she glances at him when she thinks he's not looking. Whatever's happening between them, it's definitely happening.

"Ten bucks says they don't make it to her car before he kisses her," Mercy whispers.

"You're on," Cash says. "Stone's too much of a gentleman. He'll wait until at least the second date."

"What makes you think there's going to be a first date?" Lee asks.

We all turn to stare at him.

"Have you seen the way they look at each other?" I ask. "There's definitely going to be a first date."

"Twenty says he asks her within the week," Mercy adds.

"I'll take that bet," Duck says from his corner. "Stone's been burned before. He'll take his time."

As we make our own way to the parking garage a few minutes later, I think about the evening—about new life and new possibilities, about family and love and the way everything can change in an instant.

"Penny for your thoughts," Lee says as we reach his bike.

"Just thinking about how much has changed. A year ago, I was alone in Portland, flipping houses and pretending I was happy. Now..."

"Now?"

I gesture around us—at the hospital where friends just welcomed new life, at the town that's become home, at the man who's become my everything.

"Now I have all this. A fiancé who loves me, a family that chose me, a business that's thriving, a community that's worth fighting for." I lean up to kiss him. "I have everything I never knew I wanted."

As we ride through the quiet streets of Stoneheart, past Devil's Bar where the neon sign glows welcomingly in the darkness, past the neighborhoods we helped protect from Summit's greed, I think about all the somedays stretching ahead of us.

Someday there might be a baby of our own to spoil. Someday Stone might ask Josie on that date. Someday Mercy and Cash might figure out what's between them. Someday Summit might try again.

But for now, this moment is enough. More than enough.

It's everything.

~

Thanks for reading!
Why not dive into the next in the Stoneheart MC Series
with Megan Wade's Burned in Stone....

Want more?

Check out EvieMitchell.com for a bonus scene featuring Lee and Kya!

ABOUT EVIE MITCHELL

Fierce Romance
Evie Mitchell is a thirty-something romance author (she/her/hers) who loves tales of fierce romance.
She lives with a chronic illness and often writes disability-inclusive romance.
Her loves include steamy romance novels, her husband, their THREE sausage dogs (heaven help her), and her ever-growing collection of book-related mugs.

You can catch Evie at the below.

Join Evie's reader group:
https://www.facebook.com/groups/EvieMitchells
GreedyReaders

Follow Evie on all socials
@EvieMitchellAuthor

Visit Evie's website for her current booklist:
www.EvieMitchell.com

ALSO BY EVIE MITCHELL

All Access Series

Knot My Type

Love Flushed

Darn Knit All

Larsson Siblings

Thunder Thighs

Clean Sweep

The X-List

Reality Check

The Christmas Contract

The A-List

Capricorn Cove

The Shake-up

Double the D

Muffin Top

The Mrs. Clause

New Year, Knew You

Double Breasted

As You Wish

You Sleigh Me

Meat Load

Resolution Revolution

Dogg Pack

Puppy Love

Bad English

The Frock Up

Pier Pressure

Trick or Trent

New Year's Faye

Reigning Hearts

The Marriage Claim

Silent Knight

Men of Trinity Bay

Kink in the Road

Nameless Souls MC

Runner

Wrath

Ghost

Shield

Elliot Security

Rough Edge

Bleeding Edge

www.ingramcontent.com/pod-product-compliance
Lightning Source LLC
Chambersburg PA
CBHW010020200726
48283CB00015B/3182